CONTROLLING
THE PAST

A CONTROL SERIES NOVEL

ANNA EDWARDS

Sara

This isn't the end

Anna Edward

www.AuthorAnnaEdwards.com

This is a work of fiction. Names, characters, places, and incidents are a product of the author's imagination. Locales and public names are sometimes used for atmospheric purposes. Any resemblance to actual people, living or dead, or to businesses, companies, events, institutions, or locales is completely coincidental.

Warning: This book contains sexually explicit scenes, adult language, and may be considered offensive to some readers. This book is for sale to adults only, as defined by the laws of the country in which you made your purchase.

Disclaimer: Please do not try any sexual practice without the guidance of an experienced practitioner. Neither the publisher nor the author will be responsible for any loss, harm, injury, or death resulting from the use of the information contained in this book.

Cover Design by www.CharityHendry.com
Logo Design by Charity Hendry
Editing by Tracy Roelle
Formatting by Charity Hendry and Anna Edwards
Proofreading by: Sheena Taylor

Controlling the Past/ Anna Edwards -- 1st ed.
ISBN 978-1724155610

Important note from the author:

Please note this book is set in England. The age of consent for sexual activity of any orientation in the UK, regardless of whether male or female, is sixteen. Laws for other countries maybe different, but this book is set in England and adheres to the rules of that country.

Please enjoy.

Dedication:

To Lucy, this book is about family and siblings.
I know you are far away, but you'll never stop
being my little sister. xx

CONTENTS

PART ONE 1

PROLOGUE.. 3

CHAPTER ONE.. 9

CHAPTER TWO 15

CHAPTER THREE... 21

CHAPTER FOUR 31

CHAPTER FIVE 39

CHAPTER SIX.. 49

CHAPTER SEVEN... 59

CHAPTER EIGHT... 69

CHAPTER NINE 75

CHAPTER TEN 81

PART TWO... 87

CHAPTER ELEVEN.. 89

CHAPTER TWELVE 99

CHAPTER THIRTEEN.. 109

CHAPTER FOURTEEN 117

CHAPTER FIFTEEN... 131

CHAPTER SIXTEEN.. 139

CHAPTER SEVENTEEN 149

CHAPTER EIGHTEEN....................................... 157

CHAPTER NINETEEN....................................... 165

CHAPTER TWENTY.. 171

CHAPTER TWENTY-ONE................................. 179

EPILOGUE... 193

THE CONTROL SERIES 203

GLACIAL BLOOD SERIES................................. 205

DARK SOVEREIGNTY 207

PREVIEW OF LEGACY OF SUCCESSION 209

ABOUT ANNA EDWARDS................................ 217

CONNECT WITH ANNA EDWARDS 219

MEET ANNA EDWARDS.................................. 221

PART ONE

Pete

1973 - FORTY-FIVE YEARS AGO

The melodic chime of the ice-cream van sang out, and seven-year-old Pete North placed his sand covered hand over his father's slightly pink bare chest. "Can I have an ice-cream please?"

They'd been at the beach near Broadstairs in Kent for a few hours, now, and the entire time his father had 'rested his eyes' under the burning intensity of the sunshine. It was an exceptionally hot day for England, and Pete knew his father would regret not covering himself in suntan lotion. Mind you, he wasn't sure there was much left in the bottle after his mother had smothered on the vile white, gloopy liquid. "Dad, please."

His father groaned and sat up.

"I thought you were building a sandcastle?"

"I finished it." He looked proudly over at the colossal structure, resting a bit further down the beach near the sea. It was his best work ever. Maybe, one day he could build a proper building.

Pete's mother poked her nose out from behind the book she was reading—something called, 'All things bright and beautiful by James Herriot'. "That's groovy son. Ken, I'll have a cream soda, please." Before his father could answer, Mrs North had settled her attention back to the book.

Pete's father got to his feet, and picking up his bell bottom trousers, which were lying on the sand, he searched in the pockets, and pulled out his wallet.

"What type of ice-cream do you want?" his father asked him as Pete also got to his feet and wiped his hands on his mum's kaftan.

"I want one of those with the chocolate in it. The '99' one."

His father rolled his eyes.

"I've no idea why they call them that. They've been called '99' since before I was born, and it has nothing to do with the price."

"It does seem a bit silly." He reached up with a pudgy hand and took his father's. "Mum, you're on sandcastle watch. Make sure the sea doesn't get it."

"Sure thing," his mum called from behind the book and fanned herself with it. Pete knew straightaway that if the sea came anywhere near his castle, it would be demolished. His mother loved her books and spent a great deal of time lost in them. He sometimes wondered what they contained but had decided long ago it was woman's business, and he was best to stay out of it. Girls were yucky things–they didn't like to play with worms or make mud pies. Where was the fun in that? He only needed one woman in his life, and she was his mother!

He trundled along, the sand kicking up as he struggled to keep pace with the bigger man's steps. His father bent down and scooped him up into his arms. The journey to the ice-cream van was much quicker this way, and they waited patiently until it was their turn.

"A '99', a cream soda, and I'll have..." His father paused in thought.

"Why don't you have a *Zoom*, Daddy? You like them."

"Yes, good thinking." His father tapped him on the nose. "I'll have a *Zoom*, please."

The ice-cream seller, whose sideburns joined up with his moustache, turned to prepare Pete's '99'. His father put him down on the ground and opened his wallet while Pete looked around. There were so many people at the beach today. He was sure most of the inner-city suburbs had ventured out to catch a few rays of sunshine. Varied musical tastes merged together: Elton John, Wings, Paul Simon,

Roberta Flack and The Rolling Stones competed for the loudest sound of the summertime. He laughed at the awful noise all the different genres made.

"Here you are," his father said and handed him the vanilla ice-cream, which had a chocolate flake sticking out of it. Pete stuck his tongue out and gave it a long lick. Delicious, he thought to himself. He opened his mouth and was taking a bite of the flake when he noticed a little girl standing opposite them. She went to lick her own chocolate ice-cream, but it was already half melted and slid off onto the floor. Her face fell, and her bottom lip jutted out over the top one, trembling with her distress.

"Daddy." She tugged on the trousers of the man standing next to her. "I lost my ice-cream."

The man looked down and let out a long groan.

"Miranda, what did I tell you? You have to be more careful."

The little girl sniffed back the tears, forming in her eyes.

"I'm sorry. I was careful, but the ice-cream was melting, and it slipped."

"Probably, because you were staring into space and not eating the thing. Well, you can go without. I've had enough. It's too hot here and full of undesirables. We're going home.... Augusta," he called to a well-dressed and rather hot looking woman, standing nearby.

"Charles don't be so mean to the poor darling. It wasn't her fault!" the woman exclaimed. Pete found his tongue coming out and licking his ice-cream of its own accord while watching everything unfold

"Enough," the man spoke again, and the woman silenced. "I'll wait in the car. You clean her up before she comes back. I don't want the leather getting sticky."

The man stomped off, and the little girl burst into tears.

"I'm sorry, Mummy. I didn't mean to drop it."

"I know, darling. You know what your father's like. He's not good around so many people like this. Come on, let's follow him."

The woman wiped away the girl's tears, but they kept falling.

"That was my first ever ice-cream. I really liked it."

Pete pulled his '99' away from his mouth and looked down at it.

"Wait," he called out as the girl and her mother started to walk off. They stopped and turned to look at him. "Here." He went over to them and offered the girl his ice-cream. At first, she hesitated to take it, looking up at her mother and then back at him. Her eyes were the brightest blue he'd ever seen, richer in colour than the sea he'd swam in earlier. "Please," he coaxed.

"Thank you." She reached out and took the ice-cream and had a lick of it before offering it back to him.

"No, you keep it." Her eyes went wide with surprise. "Just make sure you wash your hands before you get in your dad's car. Mine's just the same with his seats. They forget how messy we can be as kids, and once they have us, it's impossible to keep anything clean."

The little girl laughed, and Pete heard a chuckle from her mother as well.

"Say thank you to the young boy, Miranda," Augusta ordered.

"Thank you...um...I don't know your name."

"It's Peter, Pete North. That's my dad, Ken North." He pointed to where his father had finished paying and was watching them.

"Thank you, Pete. I'd better go." She took a long lick of the ice-cream, and he suddenly regretted his decision. But only a little bit because Miranda's tears had dried up, and she had a smile on her face as wide as the colossal moat he'd built for his castle.

Miranda took her mother's hand and skipped off happily with her. Pete rubbed his tummy when it gurgled. The ice-cream van put on its music and drove away. He frowned.

"Here." His dad handed him the *Zoom*. It wasn't a '99' with a chocolate flake, but he wasn't going to turn down the sugary treat. "You did a really good thing. I'm proud of you."

"It was nothing." Pete shoved the *Zoom* in his mouth and slobbered all over it, so his dad couldn't change his mind and ask for it back. "Her dad was mean, and I didn't like to see her crying."

"Get used to it, son. It happens with all women." Pete's father ruffled his hair as they headed back to the spot on the beach where his mother still lay, reading her book.

"I'll marry her, one day," Pete exclaimed as he sat on the edge of their picnic blanket.

"Marry who?" his mother asked.

"The girl I just helped." He smiled and licked the *Zoom* again.

"I thought you were getting ice-cream?" His mum looked at them both confused.

"So, did I." His father shrugged. "Although I think our little boy might have found an interest in women at the same time!"

CHAPTER ONE

Miranda

1984 – THIRTY-FOUR YEARS AGO

Miranda's head drooped forward, and she quickly righted it and stared out of the window again. It was her stop soon, and she needed to make sure she stayed awake. If she missed it, her father would be so angry. He was already upset with the fact she was coming home early from boarding school and spoiling his peace. It wasn't exactly her fault, though. She'd finished her O-level exams last week, and the teachers wanted to shut her dormitory down to allow them to re-decorate. She'd much rather have stayed at school and socialised with her friends. She was an only child. Being at home would be boring. She had at least twelve weeks before she could return to school to start studying for her A-levels. It would be the longest twelve weeks of her life.

The train pulled into the station, and she checked the sign to ensure it was her stop. She didn't want to have to call her father to let him know she'd got off the train at the wrong station. Picking up her handbag and rucksack, she walked past the few people still left in her coach and found her suitcase. She pulled the handle up and wheeled it to the carriage door. When someone opened it, she jumped down and bounced the case out of the train.

"Wait, Miss Braybrooke. I'll help you." She cocked her head to look up at the person calling her. It was her father's driver.

"Hello, Mr Pearson. It's alright.... I have it."

"Hush, child. It's my job. I wouldn't want you hurting yourself. Come on."

Miranda relinquished the handle of the suitcase over to

Mr Pearson and stepped back.

"If you insist."

"I do. Put your rucksack over my shoulder as well."

She opened her mouth to argue but knew it would be useless. Mr Pearson had been her father's driver for several years, now—ever since her daddy had come into his title and money. Her father had become Lord Braybrooke when she was ten years old, and her grandfather, the previous Lord Braybrooke, had died suddenly of a heart attack. He'd suffered injuries to his chest during army combat service in World War One, and despite being very active for a further sixty years, it was always felt by Miranda and her mother he'd left them far too soon. The same was not the opinion of her father who, at the age of fifty-three, felt it was about time he inherited. She missed her grandfather every day. He was such a character, regaling her with stories from the years gone by, especially tales of what he got up to in the roaring twenties. He'd join her on long walks around the estate they lived on, and he helped her learn to ride horses at a young age. Her father had always been so strict with her. It was as if waiting to inherit had sucked the life out of him. She couldn't remember a time when she ever really saw him smile. Her grandfather, though, would have one permanently on his face.

The sound of the train's horn pulled her out of her reflections, and she followed behind Mr Pearson.

"Your father's waiting for you in the car, Miss."

"How is he?" she asked while skipping over a case left on the platform.

"The usual." Her chauffeur's response had her body deflate and the spring in her step disappear. They walked through the station and out the main entrance towards the shiny black 1984 Mercedes-Benz.

She was dressed casually in jeans, a fluorescent t-shirt, and jacket but wished she'd dressed smarter, maybe even in her pretentious school uniform. Her father was bound to criticise what she wore. Pulling the front of her jacket together, she zipped it up and hoped he wouldn't notice.

"Hop in, Miss. I'll put these in the car, and then we'll get you home. I suspect you want nothing more than a shower and something to eat." Mr Pearson popped the boot of the car and lifted her suitcase up with a puff of exertion. She knew it was heavy after carrying it across London and all the way from her exclusive girls-only school in Cambridgeshire. It was the one her grandmother had attended and was the best. She opened the door to see her father with his briefcase open on his lap and a folder of paper in his hand.

"Hello, Father." She climbed in the car and pressed a kiss to his cheek. He looked up at her, deep rooted lines of age seemed to have extended around his eyes. She tried to recall the last time she'd been home. It must have been for her sixteenth birthday in February. It was now June, so four months. Not long but he really looked to have aged. She frowned and immediately regretted it when he caught her concerned look.

"Don't look at me like that. If I'm looking tired, it's because I've had to work long hours this week managing the estate, so I can take this time off to come and get you. That school of yours is useless. I've paid them the same amount of money this term as I did for the same period last year and have got half the service."

She shrunk down into her seat.

"I'm sorry. I did ask if they would allow me to stay anywhere else, but they said it wasn't possible."

"Bloody typical. The state of education in this country! Mind you, the school was your mother's choice. It was good enough for her mother, and she was a 'Goldsmith', so it would be the best choice for you. I'll have you know the Goldsmith name isn't as big as it once was. Braybrooke is far superior, now, thanks to the associates I've made."

"You've done so well, Father. Our name is a great one."

"It is, and your useless mother hasn't given me a son to continue it. We need to consider your marriage and soon."

"Marriage?" she spat out.

"Yes, I need to start looking into the right people. We can't have you getting involved with the wrong person and making such a fool of the family name your uncle ends up claiming the title. No, we need you married as soon as possible and pushing out male heirs within a few years."

"A few years," she stuttered. "But father, I'm only sixteen. I've got my A-levels in a couple of years, and then I want to go to university. I've got so much more I want to do with my life, first."

She looked up at her father whose cheeks had patches of red spreading across them, a sure sign he was angry at her. Mr Pearson stopped him from exploding, however, when he opened the driver's door and sat down at the wheel of the car.

"Straight home, my Lord?" he addressed her father.

"Yes." The curt reply was given, and her father refocused his attention back on her. "I mean it, Miranda. I won't let my good for nothing, anarchist brother have this title. You'll do as you are told, and you'll like it. I've given you the best life you could ever wish for. You've not wanted for anything, and you'll damn well do as you are told. No arguments." He threw the folder of papers back into his briefcase and slammed it shut before crossing his arms over his chest. "You're sixteen now, the time for childish follies is at an end. Now, you grow up." Her father turned his head to look out the car window and thereby ended the conversation. Miranda also looked away and stared out at the countryside of Surrey as it whizzed past the window. There'd always been so much competitiveness between her father and his brother, Henry. Uncle Henry wasn't interested in the title of Lord Braybrooke, far from it. He was happy exploring the world, and all things associated with the techno pop explosion, which was a sight to behold, considering he was nearly sixty. The title was more likely to go back a generation further to her grandfather's brother, if she didn't produce a male heir by the time her father died. Besides, even with the evidence of his ageing, she suspected her father wouldn't be checking out on life anytime soon.

The words that hit her the hardest, from her father's explosion, had been the ones spoken of her ungratefulness at everything he'd given her since childhood. It reminded her of an incident when she was five years old, which had shaped all future interactions with him. It may sound silly, but she'd never forgiven him for blaming her for dropping an ice-cream from her cone while at the seaside. Even worse, he'd not been a caring and understanding father who'd replaced it. No, he'd left her alone to mourn the loss of the treat until she experienced the kindness of a young stranger who gave her his. It was petty on her part to think this way, but it had been a defining moment in her relationship with her father, which had gone downhill ever since. This new assertion, on his part, that he would find her a husband and start her breeding had firmly killed any hope she had of reconciliation.

The car pulled up to their Tudor mansion, and she sighed heavily. The building was imposing, a fortress that destroyed hopes of any kind of joy. It was dark and gloomy, even the stonework gargoyles looked despondent rather than scary. Without saying another word, her father opened his door and stepped out of the car. She knew he'd disappear into his office until dinner time. Her mother appeared on the porch–if her father had looked slightly older, then her mother looked like she already had one foot in the grave. Her face was sunken, and she had dark circles around her eyes. Miranda jumped out of the car and went running up to her. Augusta Braybrooke, nee Naymouth, was nearly two decades younger than her husband. He was turning sixty in a few weeks, but she was in her forties. It was a marriage of convenience: a way for her father to obtain more money for his estates by accessing her mother's small fortune. She'd always wondered what benefits the marriage brought for her mother but never asked.

"My darling." Her mother held her closely. They were as tall as each other, now, and Miranda kissed her mother's cheek. "How did your exams go?"

"Good. I'm sure I'm going to get the grades I need to continue my education."

"I'm so happy for you. You've always been so clever. Come on, let's get you inside. I've brought afternoon tea up to your room, so after you've showered, you can tell me all about what's happened at school."

Miranda smiled. She worshipped and adored her mother. She was the one person who'd made her childhood tolerable. Sometimes, she imagined what it would be like if her father wasn't around anymore. A horrible thought that would likely get her struck down at some point and lead to her suffering an eternity in hell, but she could not help how she felt. Miranda wrapped her arm around her mother, and together, they headed off for an afternoon full of gossip. Maybe the summer wouldn't be so bad after all.

CHAPTER TWO

Pete

"Welcome, trainees. If you'd like to take a seat, our chairman will be with you shortly." The smartly dressed secretary broke out a tooth flashing smile and swayed her curvy hips as she walked out of the room. Like the two men sitting beside him who adjusted their cocks in their pants, Pete was sure he should be paying attention to the sexy little personal assistant, but he was too busy looking around the room they were in. It was an old-style building, probably from the early eighteen hundreds, and Georgian in period with large glass panelled sash windows. His body tingled with excitement at having been given this opportunity. Barrett's was one of the most prestigious banks in the UK, and thanks to his predicted excellent A-level grades, he'd been able to secure a trainee position within the firm as a banking clerk. He'd not always been financially minded. Building things was his great obsession, but he needed to make some money first before he could even begin to explore his real passion. "Hi, I'm Ian Henshaw." One of the other two men held his hand out to him. He shook it.

"Peter North."

"Albert Claridge." The other man, darker in appearance to them both, interrupted their introductions and held his hand out. Ian shook it first, and then Pete did.

"I hope all the women who work here are like that one." Ian chuckled. "It'll make looking at figures all day a lot easier."

"You'd never get anything done, if they all looked like her. You wouldn't be able to see straight!" Albert winked, grabbed his groin, and shook it.

"I think I'll just concentrate on trying to do a good job and forget the women for now." Pete looked up at the ceiling above them. It was ornately carved with a spectacular ceiling rose.

"It appears he's more interested in the décor than the women anyway." Ian laughed.

"Nerd," Albert added, but Pete ignored them.

A cough came from the doorway, and they all turned to face the older man who stood there in full morning suit, including a pocket watch.

"Mr North." The man's eyes narrowed. He spoke in clipped tones, and Pete gulped. "Would you come with me please?"

"Shit!" He heard Albert exclaim under his breath beside him. Albert and Ian both stepped back from him and reassumed their seats.

Reluctantly, placing one foot slowly in front of the other, Pete walked towards the man. He followed him out into the corridor, and down a long passageway. Pete's heart was beating fast. He'd worked so hard to get this job, and now he was wondering what had gone wrong? It had to be something serious because the face on the man as he'd told him to follow him had been thunderous. It left Pete suspecting he was about to be told his services were no longer required. He mentally ran his mind over the application form and the interview. He hadn't said anything false. He was certain of that, so what could it be?

"In here." The man pushed open a door. Pete's eyes went wide when he read the name on it – 'Ernest Barrett, Chairman' – shit, he was in big trouble. He entered the room and looked around to see it was empty. His hands were clasped in front of him, and he nervously twiddled his fingers together. The gentleman in the suit walked around him and towards a massive oak carved desk. It was lined with a faded green leather top. The piece of furniture looked almost as old as the building. "Sit down."

Pete scampered across the floor at the terse tone and sat

as quickly as his legs would allow him.

"Mr Barrett?" he stuttered in enquiry, and the older gentleman burst out laughing. Pete sat further back in his chair, looking as if he was trying to get away from a mad man but didn't have the ability to run out of the room.

"You can relax." Mr Barrett said as he took his own seat and placed his hands on the desk. Pete noticed the expensive looking signet ring he wore. "I'm sorry for the pretence of being about to fire you. I have my own way of working out who'll be the best apprentice. Congratulations, you won."

"I don't understand." Pete scrunched his face up in confusion.

"Sorry. My secretary is purposely sent in as a distraction at the greeting. Your two colleagues fell for my trap and spent most of the initial introduction with their tongues hanging out like randy dogs. You, however, paid no attention to her, even if you were distracted by my building. It shows you'll be able to focus on the job rather than chasing the skirts we have to offer in the office."

"Oh. I do like women, though." Pete felt he needed to tell Mr Barratt. He didn't have anything against homosexuality—in fact, he'd explored that side of his sexuality a couple of times, as did so many of his peers, but he'd concluded he preferred women. He was certain of that.

"I'm sure you do. The difference is you won't allow them to become a distraction, and that's why you'll be working closely with me."

"Closely with you." His mouth fell open at the opportunity he was being presented with. Mr Barratt was one of the most famous bankers in the country. He was on the front page of many a newspaper due to his incredible financial planning. He was widely sought after by the rich and famous to not only take care of their money but also to double it with investments and interest. The current financial climate wasn't the best: the threat of strikes and changes in government looked set to lead the country into a period of austerity. If you wanted to survive, you needed Mr Barratt's advice and here he was being offered the chance to train directly under him. He was gobsmacked into silence.

"Yes, you'll work with me on some of the biggest clients the bank has. I'm going to get you started straight away by throwing you in the deep in with Lord Charles Braybrooke's account. I shall be meeting him in a few weeks, and I want you to study every inch of his monetary position and develop some recommendations. What do you say?"

"I...er...can I pinch myself to check I'm not dreaming?" he replied and squeezed a piece of skin on the back of his hand.

Mr Barrett let out his bellowing laugh again and got to his feet. He went over to a desk in the corner of his room and picked up a wad of papers and folders, a foot in height.

"I'm going to like you." Mr Barratt came back to the desk and placed the papers in front of him. This is what you need to read through. The Braybrookes have been clients of ours since the bank was started by my five times great-grandfather back in the seventeen hundreds. Lord Braybrooke is one of the biggest clients we have, and your interaction will be important in continuing that relationship. I cannot stress how vital it is you really read everything here because you must understand it all. You'll need to research current financial models and future risks. My assistant will be able to help you with that. You'll need to run any models you choose to adopt through the computers we have on the ground floor to ensure the probabilities of risk to the client are not too great. We aren't in the habit of making our clients bankrupt." Mr Barratt pushed the papers towards him. "You'll have a desk across the way with my assistant. Now, if you understand what I expect from you, then I suggest you start reading."

Pete got to his feet, picked up the massive pile of papers, and tucked them under his arm.

"I understand everything, Sir. Thank you for this opportunity. I won't let you down."

Mr Barratt sat back in his chair and lit up a cigar.

"I know you won't. I see a lot of myself in you. I think we'll work well together. Any questions just ask."

Pete nodded his head in gratitude, and stepping out of the office, he pulled the door closed and rested back against it. His heart was still beating so fast. He couldn't believe he was being given this chance. It would be the making of his career. His mum would be so proud when he told her.

Mr Barrett's secretary beckoned him into her office with a waggle of her finger. She was sexy, and he was a hot-blooded male, but she just didn't do it for him. He had it in his head he needed to succeed first with his career. He was certain the right woman was out there for him—one day, he'd meet her and know immediately she was his. From that moment, they'd never be apart again. He wouldn't let her get away. But for now, he had a lot of reading to do and wasn't going to let Mr Barrett down. He went into the room with the secretary and noticed there was a desk already set up for him. He took a seat at it and started reading. A few moments later, Albert entered the room carrying a pile of papers. Pete looked up and nodded at him in greeting.

"You got a client as well?" Pete asked.

"Client?" Albert strode moodily towards the photocopier and placed the papers down. Pete sucked in his lip when it dawned on him Albert had been given a different kind of task. The brown-haired man picked up the first piece of paper and fed it through the photocopier. He repeated the process with a sullen look on his face. Ian came into the room next carrying a tray of tea and coffee. Pete lowered his head into his paperwork and smiled. He was going to like this job –it would be the making of him!

CHAPTER THREE

Miranda

"Miranda, will you hurry up?" her father shouted up the grand staircase to her. She pinned the last strands of her thick brown locks into place within her bun and pulled on the silk gloves her maid had laid out.

"Coming," she called down the stairs while reaching for her handbag and slipping her sparkling black court shoes on. In a flash, she ran out of her room, the door slamming shut behind her, and down the stairs to where her father paced impatiently.

"Women," he sighed with exasperation. "It takes you forever to get ready, and you still look a state when you say you're done."

Miranda looked down at her designer A-line dress in a teal colour. She thought it suited her colouring well, but obviously not.

"Should I change?" she asked.

"I don't have time for that. Get in the car. Why I agreed with your mother to take you today is beyond me. All you'll do is get in the way and send my blood pressure through the roof. And no doubt, she'll spend the day frittering more of my money away with beauty treatments that have little hope of working."

Miranda didn't respond to her father's diatribe. Instead, she hurried into the car and disappeared to the world inside her head for the journey to London. It was nicer in there where she had a father who respected and loved her.

The ride to London didn't take long with Mr Pearson weaving through the traffic. She was sure he should've been a racing driver instead of a chauffeur. He winked at her when he opened the door, and she smiled back before taking her father's arm. She looked up at the imposing building in front of them.

"Where are we?" she enquired.

"Barratt's Bank."

Her father's reply was curt, so she decided against asking him anything else. He took his briefcase from Mr Pearson, and Miranda followed him up the steps of the Georgian style building. The hubbub of the bustling streets of London disappeared when they entered through the door. A blast of icy air-conditioning hit them and washed away the heat of the British summer.

"Lord Braybrooke." A man dressed in a full morning suit stepped forward and dipped his head down in a show of courtesy. "Mr Barrett is expecting you. If you'd like to follow me this way, please."

Her father shook the man's hand firmly, to leave the poor fellow with no doubts as to who oversaw the situation.

"Miranda, keep up," her father ordered, and her court heels echoed across the wooden floors as she jogged to keep pace with the men's wide strides. They entered a lift, and it rose to the tenth floor. All the time, she watched her father's face. He was always stern, but this was something different. He was in complete business mode. Nothing or no one was going to distract him from whatever goals he had in his mind to achieve today. The lift pinged, and the men were off at a rapid pace again. She followed them as best she could, wishing she'd been allowed to wear her favourite jeans, trainers, and t-shirt instead. She didn't often get to wear casual clothes, but when she did, she had a fondness for slogans. The latest one she'd purchased told her to 'choose life'. There was so much irony in the statement she wasn't even sure where to begin to explain it, especially to her father after he'd rolled his eyes when she chose to wear it to dinner one evening. It wasn't quite the pearls and twinset he deemed appropriate.

"Miranda, for goodness sake will you stop dawdling? I don't have all day to wait around for you while you're off dreaming about fairies and god knows what else. Keep your mind focused on the task, which is putting one foot in front of the other and behaving like the lady you supposedly are."

She sighed heavily and looked down at the ground, wishing it would swallow her up. She was a constant disappointment, always had been and was likely to always be. Why couldn't she have been a boy? It would have made things so much easier.

The door to a massive boardroom was pushed open and there, sitting at the table, was the reason she was happy to be a girl. Her lady parts had suddenly awakened and were preparing themselves for the vision before her. Not the old man who greeted her father with affection but the slightly shy looking boy beside him who was regarding her. No, he wasn't a boy, definitely a man. His lip curled up into a smirk, which had her heart fluttering so fast it seemed like it would beat out of her chest. He stood and dominated the room. He must have been at least six feet plus a good couple of inches. His chest was broad in his suit, which was sculpted to his body and accentuated his narrow hips. She was salivating. He was fucking gorgeous. She'd never seen someone like him before.

"Mr Barratt." Her father's deep voice broke through her vision of the man's luscious lips, pressing against the sudden throb in her panties. "I'd like you to meet my daughter, Miranda. I'm showing her the ropes today. Giving her a bit of an insight into the running of the old business."

"Miss Braybrooke." The older man stepped forward and shook her hand. He was dressed formally with a pocket watch hanging from a chain, which was attached to his trousers. "It's a pleasure to meet you. I bet you're excited to learn more about your father's finances and what the future holds for you."

Miranda opened her mouth to answer but was cut off by the bellowing laugh of her father. "Good one, Charles. I see you still have a great sense of humour. All she'll be doing in the future is bringing her husband his tea and whisky while he works hard. Speaking of which......."–Miranda watched her father turn his attention to the hunk of a man standing next to Mr Barrett – "I'll have white, two sugars, please."

Mr Barrett coughed through the awkward silence that followed her father's instructions.

"Lord Braybrooke, there's been some confusion. Mr North here is my assistant. He's being studying your files for the last two weeks and has made some excellent suggestions on how we can improve your financial position.

The features on her father's face tightened, and his eyes darkened with anger.

"I don't pay you to have your assistants work on my files. I pay for your services and yours alone. Am I not the most important client you have? I would never have been treated this way when your father ran my account."

"Lord Braybrooke." Mr North stepped forward and inserted himself into the conversation. "I can assure you, Sir, Mr Barrett has worked closely with me at all times. He thought a fresh pair of eyes would be beneficial to your future prosperity."

"I don't give a fuck what he thinks or what work you've done together. I pay to work with Mr Barrett alone. and if he can't do that, then I shall leave right now and take my business to someone who'll treat me with the respect I deserve and not farm out my important financial future to a boy fresh out of nappies."

"Lord Braybrooke, Mr North is a trusted employee."

"I'm walking." Her father picked up the briefcase, which he'd placed on the table to shake hands, and made for the open doorway.

Miranda looked to where Mr Barrett and the young man, who still had her panties in a twist, stood. The older of the two looked stressed and sad at the same time. The younger picked up a folder, which looked to contain several handwritten notes, and gestured for the other to take it.

"Miss Braybrooke, should we leave Mr Barrett and your father to discuss business in peace? We'll only hinder them." Mr North urged the older man to take the folder one last time, and he reluctantly did. "Lord Braybrooke, I apologise for the confusion. I'll return with your tea shortly. I'll ensure Miss Braybrooke is taken care of while you work with my employer."

Miranda looked to where her father was watching what was unfolding. He had a supercilious look on his face, which she would love nothing more than to wipe clean away with a hard-thrown punch. Instead, she pulled her handbag a little higher up on her shoulder, stuck her nose into the air, and glided past her father and out the door. She did so without so much as a goodbye or acknowledgement that this course of action was either for or against his wishes. She was furious. He'd been rude and disrespectful. Footsteps came up behind her, and a hand was placed into the small of her back. Warmth tingled through her body, and she let out an almost silent moan of satisfaction.

"I'll take you to Mr Barrett's office, Miss. You can wait in there for your father. I hope I read the signs right, and you'd also prefer to be out of the room."

She slammed to a halt and turned to face him directly.

"My father was just abominably rude to you, yet you were thinking more about getting me out of the room than smacking him in the face?"

A cheeky smirk crossed the man's face. "I wouldn't say that. I've worked long hours on the project for the last two weeks. I'm probably running on adrenaline rather than sleep. If I didn't like my job so much, I'm afraid your father would likely have blood streaming from his nose, right now."

Miranda placed her hand against her mouth and giggled into it, trying to silence her amusement at the situation. Her blood still boiled deeply within, but she was glad she wasn't in the boardroom listening to the boring conversation the other two men were no doubt engaged in.

Another young man poked his head around a doorway and frowned at them,

"I thought you were in the Braybrooke meeting?" the newcomer asked.

"Change of plans. I'll be looking at Miss Braybrooke's finances as well. Her father wants her to start planning for her future." The other man looked her up and down, and she was certain she saw him lick his lips.

"Lucky bastard," he muttered.

"That I am," Mr North added and opened a door for her. "By the way, Albert, can you arrange for a white tea with two sugars for Lord Braybrooke? I'd keep your head down when you go in there to deliver it, though. He's a bit of a tyrant."

"Shit." Albert groaned and disappeared. She and Mr North entered a massive room decked out in the finest Chippendale furniture.

"Please, take a seat. Is there anything I can get you to drink? I'm Peter, Pete for short, by the way"

"Miranda." She shook her head. "No thank you, on the drink, I'm good. I want to apologise again for my father's behaviour. I wish I could say it was his age, but he's been like it ever since I can remember."

"That must make things hard for you?" He motioned for her to take a seat. She did, and he sat opposite her at the big oak desk in the middle of the room.

"I've not known any different. He's always been that way with me. One of my earliest memories is of him shouting at me on the beach because I dropped the ice-cream out of my cone." Pete leaned forward on the desk at her words, his brows furrowed together with intense interest. "If it wasn't for a kind boy giving me his ice-cream that day, I would have gone without. You don't do that to a five-year-old year girl."

"Broadstairs," Pete announced with a massive grin on his face.

"I'm sorry? She placed her handbag down on the floor and stared at him. Her own brows knitting together in confusion this time.

"You had, let me think.... it was a long time ago....." He bit his lip in deep thought, and it slowly started to dawn on her who he was. What were the odds? It must have been millions if not billions to one. "I had a '99', but you had a chocolate ice-cream. I've always remembered how happy you were when I offered you my half-licked cone with a bite out of the top of the flake. I'm not sure your mum was overly impressed. I think she probably saw the germs I was sharing." He laughed, and she joined in.

"I can't believe it was you. How is it possible?"

"The luck of the gods, I think."

"I like the gods. You've grown up a bit since then." Miranda blushed when the words came out of her mouth. She hadn't meant to be so blunt.

"I can say the same about you," he teased her.

"Thank you again for giving me your ice-cream."

"It wasn't a problem."

"And I really am sorry my father won't let you be in on the meeting. I'm sure you've worked extremely hard to impress him."

"A little." Pete shrugged his shoulders, and she got the feeling he was downplaying the task he'd undertaken and the disappointment he was experiencing. "Your father spoke of a future husband. Are you in a relationship?"

She shook her head in the negative.

"No, but I have a feeling he's going to be lining up the potential candidates for me....no scrap that, for him to choose from soon."

"This is the eighties not the Victorian era. You can choose your own husband. If you even want one."

She slumped down into the chair and started to fiddle with a button on her dress.

"Do I look like I'm living in the eighties? I'm sixteen, seventeen in a few months, and I'm dressed like someone from the fifties. I'd kill to wear a shell suit like other people of my age, but I can only do that when hidden in the privacy of my own home, so nobody can see."

"Your father's a tyrant."

"He wants what's best for me, I guess."

The man opposite her raised a quizzical eyebrow. "Ok, he's a bit of a bully," she finally conceded.

"I've got an idea." Pete jumped to his feet and went across the room to check the door was shut properly.

"What are you doing?" she asked, her skin suddenly feeling a little clammy at the prospect of being shut away alone with a man who wasn't a relative of hers. Her father wouldn't like it.

Pete came back to the desk and opened one of the drawers. He pulled out a mini radio and plugged it into a socket underneath the desk. He flipped a switch and static filled the room. She instantly covered her ears against the loud noise.

"Sorry. Mr Barratt always untunes it after he's finished playing it because he thinks nobody'll know he's listening to modern music. Pointless, since we can all hear it in the next room because he's going a little deaf and has it up so loud." Pete's laugh was so infectious that she got to her feet and came around to his side of the desk with a giggle on her lips. He flipped his finger across the switch to retune the radio, and she watched, wondering what that finger would feel like playing with her body. What was it about this man that put her mind straight into the gutter? He found a station and the latest rock music blasted out from the speaker. He quickly turned it down a bit and held his hand out to her.

"Dance?"

"Please." She took his hand, and he pulled her into the hard lines of his body. He must do plenty of exercise because underneath the suit, it seemed, he had the body to show for it. The song changed to, 'You Give Love a Bad Name' by Bon Jovi, and they held hands while rocking out and singing almost but not quite at the top of their voices. She head banged wildly at the chorus, unravelling the neat bun on her head.

They were both laughing so much as one upbeat song

followed another, and her side hurt from a possible pulled muscle. She was unsure whether it related to the laughing or the rumbustious dancing they were doing. The instantly recognisable opening guitar riff of 'When Doves Cry' by Prince played, and Pete pulled her into him, and that's how they stayed for the whole of her favourite song. Just the two of them caught-up together in the emotion of the words and the freeing experience he was giving her.

"That day at the beach, I said something to my father after you left." Pete reached for a stray strand of her hair and tucked it behind her ear.

"What?" she asked looking up into his deep blue eyes. "I told him one day I'll marry you." She gasped. "It was a childish comment at the time but seeing you here today"– he pulled her tighter into his arms– "I'm thinking maybe I knew what fate had in store for us, even then."

The door handle rattled, and they pulled quickly apart from each other as Mr Barratt and her father strode into the room. Pete reached for the radio and turned it off.

"Here you are," her father grumbled. "We've been looking for you."

She tried to form sensible words to explain what they'd been doing, but her body felt like jelly, and her mind was a pool full of nothingness.

"I thought it best to keep Miss Braybrooke away from the main floor, Mr Barratt." –Pete stepped forward– "I know both Ian and Albert are around and the issues you have with them."

Mr Barratt nodded at him approvingly.

"Good idea."

"I hope you don't mind, we put the radio on and were looking over some of your financial books. Miranda was particularly interested in this one." He grabbed a book from a nearby shelf and handed it to her. She read the title.

"The theory of investment value." She smiled up at the two older gentlemen in the room. "It seems a riveting read."

"That it is," –Her father stepped forward and ripped the

book from her hand– "but too high brow for you. House-hold husbandry would better suit your future."

He discarded the book on the shelf like a poisoned chal-ice filled with hopes and dreams she could never have, because she was a woman.

"I have another meeting at midday. Come, we need to depart."

Her heart sped up. She was going to have to leave Pete, and she had no way of contacting him again. If Mr Barratt fired him because of her father, there'd be no way she could find him again. Her palms started to sweat with the realisation this could be the last time she ever saw him.

"I'm coming," she responded to her father and picked up her handbag. Pete stood off to the side, his face marked with lines of worry and fear. He felt exactly the same. Something was happening between them –it had started all those years ago, on the beach, and fate had brought them back together again.

Her father turned away and stomped out of the door, calling her name over his shoulder. Mr Barratt followed close behind. Miranda took the short time she had left to grab a piece of paper from the bank owner's desk and scrib-ble down her home address on it. She thrust it into Pete's hand, and as she turned to run out of the room, she called back to the man now staring down at her address, "If you're going to marry me, you'll have to date me first. Find a way."

CHAPTER FOUR

Pete

It had seemed like an ingenious way of getting to meet with Miranda, at the time. But as Pete waited for the chauffeur, Mr Pearson, to deliver her to the rendezvous point, he was starting to worry. What if the driver had informed her father of what was happening? Miranda would no doubt get into big trouble. They'd managed to speak a few times over the last week, since meeting again for the first time in more than ten years. She had one of those massive great big mobile phones, which were becoming all the rage amongst the elite, so he'd called her, when he could, from a phone booth down the road from his house. The chats were limited mainly to sharing basic getting to know each other facts: favourite things, food, drink, colours, TV shows. Snippets about their lives growing up and what their hopes and aspirations for the future were. He still couldn't believe she was the same girl he'd given his ice-cream to on the beach. Either it was fate intervening and bringing them together, or he'd been so good in another life he was being granted the best of luck in this one.

He tapped his foot impatiently and looked down the road for any sign of a car approaching. Nothing. The suburban street he was waiting on was deathly quiet, which was a rarity in the ever-expanding metropolitan city that London had become. She wasn't coming. The damned driver had shafted them, and Miranda would be prevented from going out in future or shipped away from him never to be seen again. His shoulders slumped, and he fell back against the wall behind him. He really liked Miranda. When she'd walked into the office, she'd appeared like a vision of angelic beauty. She was a goddess in her teal dress with sensible shoes, and her hair neatly pulled back to show the perfect features of her face: full lips that were very kissable, and bright eyes that hinted at an air of mischief lying beneath them. He'd learned about her love of music during their dancing episode. It matched his own. He felt the despondency flooding through his body.

A car horn beeped, and he looked up. It was the car he'd seen Miranda climb into when leaving the bank. He pushed off the wall and waved it down. The driver swerved into the curb and came to a halt directly in front of him. The back door opened, and Miranda jumped out. She was dressed in a pair of distressed faded jeans and a T-shirt, which stated she was 'living the dream'. He chuckled.

"Hi. I'm so sorry I'm late. My father left behind schedule to go to the airport, and then Mr Pearson got stuck in traffic on the way back to get me. It's the only time in his life my father has ever been late. Do you forgive me?" Miranda looked up at him with puppy dog eyes. Just that look was enough to make him forgive her anything. His cock shifted in his jeans, and he willed it to stay down. The last thing he needed was a raging erection.

"Forgiven." He stepped forward and took her hand. A cough came from behind them. He'd forgotten her driver.

"I'll call you when I'm ready for you to come and get me, if that's ok?" Miranda turned to her driver and willed him not to show her up. The desperation was written all over her face.

"Where are you going?" Mr Pearson ignored her and focused his attention on Peter.

"A TV show recording." Pete pulled tickets from his pocket and showed them to the enquiring driver. Miranda squealed when she saw the name of the show. Mr Pearson flinched.

"Top of the Pops. Seriously! Oh My God, you got us tickets."

Pete nodded. "Mr Barratt felt guilty that I'd worked so hard on your father's account but wasn't actually allowed to attend the meeting. He gave me a little bonus, and I bought the tickets with it."

"I've wanted to go on that show for so long. I watch it religiously. I can't believe it." Miranda let go of his hand and wrapped her arms around his neck and pressed a kiss to his lips. She must have realised what she was doing too late for she pulled back and looked guiltily at the floor while biting her lip.

"Sorry," she whispered.

"It's ok," he reassured her.

Mr Pearson coughed again, and Miranda took a step further away from Pete.

"What about after?"

"After?" He cocked his head towards the driver.

"Do I collect her here or somewhere else?"

Pete looked over to Miranda.

"Here," she murmured, and Pete saw the satisfied smile spread over Mr Pearson's face.

Pete stepped forward

"I can assure you Miranda's safe, sir. I simply want to get to know her better."

"There's a pie and mash shop down the road. I'll go and get something to eat. You have your phone?" Miranda nodded and tapped her handbag. "Call me if you need me."

"I will. Thank you, Mr Pearson."

"Go have fun, you two. A part of me is jealous. I enjoy Top of the Pops as well."

The chauffeur jumped back in the car and disappeared down the street before they could respond.

"I can't believe you did this?"

"I know how much you love music, and I'm told Frankie Goes to Hollywood is performing tonight."

"NO!" Miranda screamed again. "Paul Rutherford's so cute."

"Hey!" he teased. "I thought you were here on a date with me not to lust over a pop star."

"I am. It's just.... You know."

He jabbed her lightly in the ribs. "I know. Come on, the show starts soon."

He took Miranda's hand and led her through to the entrance of the studio where he showed their tickets. They then stored Miranda's lightweight jacket and handbag with the concierge before entering the studios. Pete watched Miranda. She looked a lot older than her almost seventeen years. Her jeans were skin tight and accentuated the luscious curves of her hips and arse. Her T-shirt was fluorescent pink and tight around her breasts. Damn, she's hot. She turned to face him, and he couldn't help but smile at how her appearance, now, differed from the way she'd looked at the office the other day. The prim and proper Lord's daughter was gone. Her twinset and pearls replaced by a black rubber necklace, and the tight bun hairstyle now a vivacious backcombed creation with crimped sections throughout and pink streaks, matching her t-shirt.

"What?" She interrupted his thoughts. "Am I dressed wrong?"

He shook his head.

"No, you're beautiful. Perfect."

She blushed a little.

"You're going to embarrass me."

He leaned forward and pressed his lips to hers and they kissed for a second time that evening.

"Thank you for agreeing to come on this date with me."

He wrapped his arm around her waist and pulled her against him.

"Thank you for finding a way to make it happen."

Music started up around them, and the opening melody of the show blasted out from the speakers. It was recognisable all over the UK now, and the fact he was actually here, sent shivers down his spine. He'd grown up, as Miranda had, watching the show every Thursday evening. Just like her, he'd made a mix tape every Sunday evening of the music from the 'Top Forty' charts on the radio. It was what people of his age did. He'd done it in his youth, and he wasn't planning on stopping now he was an adult. Music would always be a love of his, and he was glad he'd found someone to share it with.

The voice of Steve Wright, the presenter, rang out around the studio as he announced the first act, 'The Bluebells'. Miranda squealed with delight, and they rushed forward with the rest of the crowd to dance. He made sure to keep her close to him for the rest of the evening, especially when Frankie Goes to Hollywood came on. The studio was busy because the show was one of the most popular on television. When the final act finished, an exhausted Miranda collapsed against him.

"I need something to drink. I don't think I've ever danced so much," she said breathlessly.

"There's a café down the road. Shall we go there?"

"Please."

They collected her coat and bag, and he made her check everything was still in it and nothing had been stolen. When satisfied, he placed his arm around her shoulder and led them out of the building.

"Thank you for bringing me here. It's the most fun I've had in my life. Boy, that sounds really sad." Her face deflated, and he wanted nothing more than to take the hurt away from her.

"Well, we'll have plenty more years of fun to experience together."

"You meant what you said about having a future together?"

"Hell yes. Fate, Miranda, has brought us back together, and I'm not letting you get away again."

He pushed open the door to a café, and they took two seats by the window. A waitress immediately appeared, and they ordered two coffees and two slices of their cake of the day—black forest gateaux. Pete dove his fork into the chocolate devilment and watched Miranda. The sadness hadn't lifted from her. Her eyes had dulled from those that had been glistening with excitement during the recording of the

TV show.

"Talk to me," he encouraged. She looked up from where she was pushing a piece of the cake around her plate.

"I don't want to hurt you."

"Why would you?"

He reached out with his free hand and wrapped his fingers around hers resting on the table.

"Because of my father. I don't think my life is my own to decide what I'll do. I'm destined to be a trophy wife to fulfil my father's desire to further his family name. He doesn't want my uncle getting the title, and a female can't inherit it, so he'll manipulate me into marrying his man of choice."

"His choice not being a banker's assistant who's not even worthy of looking at his financial papers."

"Exactly."

Miranda placed her fork down on the table and pushed the uneaten cake away before letting go of his hand and standing.

"I should go. You've given me an experience I'll never forget, and I don't want to lead you on as a result."

She made to flee from the restaurant, but he was quicker and was on his feet and grabbed her hand in an instant. The coffee cups rattled at the sudden movement.

"Don't go," he rasped.

"Pete, please." Miranda turned back to face him. Tears filled her eyes. He didn't let go of her wrist but with his free hand wiped away a tear as it tumbled down her cheek.

"I won't let you walk out of my life. There may be hurt down the road, but that's relationships. They're hard work. I've learned from watching my own parents, but as long as we don't give up, we'll beat the doubters and any opposition."

"I can't ever hope to beat my father. Don't you see that? I've never once gone against him in my life."

"But you have."

"What?" Miranda relaxed a little, and he loosened the firm grip he had on her wrist but still kept contact with her skin.

"You're defying him now. You're taking your life into your own hands and making decisions for yourself. If you'd asked him for permission to come on a date with me, what would he have said?"

"No."

"Exactly."

"That's different."

"It's not." He shook his head at her.

"I won't be able to continue telling lies to him. What if I fall in love with you? It's going to hurt so badly when I have to walk away, because I know he won't let me be with you?"

"Then don't let him win. Your father's just that, Miranda, simply your father. We don't live in the dark ages. This is the eighties, and we're free to make our own decisions. Don't let him dictate your future. If you want a career, go for it. You want to be a doctor, go to university because from what I know about you, you're intelligent enough to pass the exams. But, if you want to be a lady of leisure and live off your husband, I'll work as damn hard as I can to make sure I can provide you with that sort of life. You've just got to have the guts to say no to your father. If he's half the man he should be, then he'll support any decisions you make. If not, he'll chuck you out, but would it be such a loss? Are you so engrained into the lifestyle you were brought up in that you can't see beyond it and consider another?"

"That's not fair. I'm not in love with the privilege I have, but it's all I've ever known. I wouldn't know the first thing about surviving on my own."

"But that's it. You don't have to."

He led her back to the table and forced her to sit back down.

"Even if you didn't want a relationship with me, I think I've come into your life for a reason. It's the same principle as with the ice-cream. What your father has taken away from you, I can give back. I can help you find a life when now, as you say, you have none. Walk away from this opportunity, Miranda, if it's what you truly want to do, but if it isn't, then I suggest you eat your cake."

Pete watched his table partner intently while he resumed his own seat and started eating again. She looked between the door and the cake, back to the door and then the cake again. Eventually, she shut her eyes and letting out a long sigh, she opened her sapphire orbs, picked up the fork, and took a mouthful of cake.

"It's time to live, to love, to experience everything...together."

CHAPTER FIVE

Miranda

It had been a month since she'd met Pete for a second time after the ice-cream incident of their youth. Her summer would be over in a month and a half, and she'd be returning to her boarding school in a few weeks to continue her education. It had been a fight with her father to allow her to do so, but eventually, she'd bargained another two years for herself. Two years in which, hopefully, she could figure out some way of getting her father to allow her to live the life she wanted and not the one he would dictate. Her time with Pete was precious. They spent most of it sitting around in her bedroom talking, after he'd snuck in through the window, because she wasn't always able to get away. Mr Pearson was fantastic when they did manage to meet for dates. The chauffeur developed a fondness for Pete, and the two men often spent time talking together during the rendezvous. Pete arranged for them to go roller skating, and to see Ghostbusters at the cinema. He was even able to organise a trip back to Broadstairs when her father was away for a few days. He spent one evening holding her hair back as she emptied the contents of her stomach down a toilet while suffering from a bug. Miranda suspected her mother knew she was seeing someone but kept it to herself, which Miranda was grateful for. Her mother was a wonderful woman, but she didn't want her to have to lie to her father, because it would only cause trouble for her mother. Her parent's relationship had died years ago. Miranda's, however, was just starting. The physical side of her liaison with Pete was becoming rather hot and heavy. They'd started to fool around a lot, but it hadn't gone any further than him getting her off with his fingers. She'd felt guilty and offered to return the favour, but he'd refused because he didn't trust himself to be around her with his cock out. She'd felt it during their make out sessions and knew it was big and pretty much always hard. It must have been uncomfortable for him in that condition. She'd gone to bed the last time he'd left her, imagining him stroking himself off to thoughts of her. It was a glorious vision, and one that, before long, had her coming with her hand down her PJ bottoms. Her maid had spoken to her about sex a few years ago, but she'd already known what it was all about from the girls at her school. Several of them had long term boyfriends and were sexually active with them. She'd not really been interested in it because sex meant men, and men just caused trouble. Although Pete was nothing like that. She knew he worshipped her, and she was at the point in their relationship where she knew she no longer wanted a life that didn't have him in it. She saw herself married to him with a little boy and girl running around their feet. That was the future she wanted, not the one her father would force upon her. She needed to speak to Pete about it because she didn't want to hide their relationship any longer. She wanted it out in the open. It would be hard to arrange to meet up when she was back at school in Cambridge, so she wanted to do whatever she could to make sure it was possible to see him every weekend.

The recognisable tap to the window had her heartbeat fluttering, and she leapt from the bed and was across the room and unfastening the window in two seconds.

"Hi." Pete smirked back at her from the tree branch he was perched on. He had a bag in his hand, and she took it from him, so he could swing himself through the open window.

He pulled her instantly into his arms, and they locked lips in a passionate kiss.

"Damn, I've missed you." It had been only two days since they'd last met, but Pete's enthusiasm for her, had her panties instantly wet. "I was going out of my mind."

"You're such a dork, sometimes." She patted his chest and opened the bag to look at what was inside. "Pick and mix." She excitedly thrust her hand into the bag and pulled out a sugar-coated cola bottle. "My favourite."

"I thought we could watch a movie with some snacks."

"I like that idea." She padded over to the TV she had in her room and switched it over to the VHS player. "I've only really got romance films, though?"

"That's ok. I brought this." He pulled a video called Octopussy out of his pocket. "It's a spy film. Yes or No?" He waggled the video in front of him with a puppy dog look on his face.

"I'm guessing you are a James Bond fan."

"A little. I'd make a good spy, don't you think?"

She threw her head back and laughed so hard her sides started to hurt. When she finally calmed down and looked at Pete, he had a wounded look on his face.

"I'm sorry. I didn't mean..." She started to laugh again.

"Didn't mean what?" His eye's darkened, and the intense look on his face sent shivers down her spine. Her body was reacting in all sorts of strange ways again. She wanted him. She wanted him moving inside her and making love to her. She knew in that moment, watching his face glow with the affection he had for her, that she was ready.

"Make love to me," abruptly came from her lips before she registered what she was saying.

Pete's eyes went wide with shock.

"Ww...what?" he stuttered.

"I want you fully. Make me yours."

"Miranda."

"Please." She stepped up and placed her hands on his chest. The desperation in her voice was evident.

"I.. I..." Pete tried desperately to find words to say no to her. She brought her finger to his lips to silence him from saying something she didn't want to hear.

"Don't reject me, please. I've never wanted something more than I want you, right now. I know you're my everything. My life, my future, my love..."

Her last word hung thickly in the air between them.

"You love me?"

"Yes. I've loved you since you gave me your ice-cream. You were right, fate has decreed we're destined for each other, and I don't want to wait anymore. I want to shout from the rooftops you're mine. I want you as much as you want me but are too scared to admit."

Pete took a long shuddering breath and looked down at the ground. Had she read the situation wrong? Did he not want her? Was he just playing with her? She took a step backwards and held her hands over her heart. It felt like it was breaking.

"No." Her voice broke on the word, but she couldn't get any more words out because Pete was on her. His mouth attached to hers, and his tongue slid in-between her lips, tasting her and taking away all the negative thoughts from her mind. He pulled back but never let go of her.

"I love you. I've wanted you forever. I've been so scared of hurting you and of you not being ready. I've known all along that you're mine. Your body, mind, and soul are joined with mine, and we'll never be apart."

He scooped her into his arms and laid her down onto the bed. His mouth found hers again, kissing and tasting her delicate flesh as if it was one of the sweets in the pick and mix bag. His hands skimmed over her body, and all her nerve endings were ignited with sensations she'd never felt before.

This was it –this was her moment.

Pete opened the zipper of the jeans she was wearing, sliding his fingers inside to reach her pussy. She was soaked and ready for him. She always was when he was around. He pushed a finger inside her and a groan escaped her mouth, leaving the man touching her body in no doubt as to her acceptance of him. He pushed another finger inside. At the same time, his thumb found her clit and started to circle it. She was breathless for him already. Her orgasm was approaching so rapidly she wanted it to crash into her but at the same time she never wanted this feeling to be over.

"Harder," she groaned, and Pete lightly bit her lip. "Please...." Where the begging was coming from, she had no idea. She'd never begged for anything in her life. She'd just accepted she wouldn't be given anything and bemoaned her situation in silence, but this was different. With the man who would soon be her bedded lover, she wanted to beg and plead and cry and scream and worship him for the way he made her feel.

Her hands came to her jeans, and she tried desperately to push them down her thighs to give him better access to the treasure between her legs.

"No," he ordered, and she froze. "I'll undress you. It's my job." The masterful way in which he spoke had her writhing further on the bed with need.

Pete pulled her jeans down her legs and helped her sit up, so he could remove her t-shirt. He pulled his own t-shirt over his head and allowed her a few moments to take in his muscular stomach, broad shoulders, and tattoo. Holy Shit! He had a tattoo, and she didn't know. He brought his lips back to hers, but she pushed him away.

"What?" He looked confused and a little scared she was changing her mind.

"Tattoo," she reassured, and he looked down to his left side of his chest where the Polynesian tattoo covered it and spread up to his right shoulder. "Beautiful." She felt like she was a dribbling mess, but she was so in awe of the intricate design.

"You like?" he asked, and she nodded, having lost the ability to form comprehensible words. "I had it done for my eighteenth birthday. My mum cried, but my dad was impressed. I want to get it all over my shoulder and down my arm one day, but I need to be careful. Tattoos don't exactly go down too well in the banking industry. Best to make sure it's kept hidden at all times." He stroked his hand over the design.

"Did it hurt?"

"A little but nothing I couldn't handle."

"It's really beautiful."

"Thank you." His eyes sparkled with devilment while he looked at her like she was lunch. It was a menu she hoped he would enjoy. "Enough talking......more clothes removing."

Miranda looked down and realised she was having a conversation with Pete in just her bra and knickers. A sudden bout of self-consciousness hit her, and she tried to cover herself up, but Pete shook his head.

"No, you're mine to explore, now. Mine to devour."

She took his hand and led him towards the bed. Slowly, she placed her hands at the clasp of her bra but remembered at the last second he'd said her clothes were his to remove. She looked at him for permission to remove it, and he nodded his approval, so she undid the bra and lowered it to the cradle of her arms. Summoning up as much of her inner sex goddess as she could, she let go of the gossamer fabric and allowed it to fall to the floor. Her perky tits, not too big and not too small she thought, were bared to the man standing in front of her, and judging by the lascivious look on his face, he liked what he saw.

"Panties." He ordered her to remove them with a flick of his head. She placed her hand in the elastic banding, which held them up, and lowered them down her svelte legs before standing up and displaying her naked body to him. She was natural down below. Some people, in a decade that was starting to see medical enhancements and beauty procedures explode, liked to have all the hair removed, but she wasn't keen on having that area so exposed. Pete reached for his own jeans and started to palm his cock through the rigid fabric.

"I knew this would be how you looked. Innocent and pure with a body built for sin."

He backed her up further, so she fell onto the bed with her legs parted and inner most parts on display for him.

"Mine." The word escaped from his mouth and seemed to come as shock to both of them.

"Yours," she repeated, stroking her finger down the length of her slit to demonstrate just how much she was his.

Pete undid the buckle of his jeans and slid them down his muscled thighs. She already knew he liked to go to the gym a couple of nights a week. He'd told her he was teased for being a wimpy kid at one stage, but then he'd found the gym and hadn't looked back. The muscle certainly looked good on him. His boxer briefs followed suit, and she gasped when his erect cock sprung free from its confines. She'd not seen one this close before. Ok, the girls at her school had shared pictures from porn magazines, but she'd never had a real-life one in front of her. It was strange but stunning at the same time. Its rigidity caused it to reach up to his belly button. In fact, his length and width was more impressive than some of the photos she'd seen. She suddenly felt a little self-conscious. This would be her first time, and something that size would have to hurt.

Pete came over to the bed, settling between her thighs with his mouth close to the cleft between her legs, his tongue came out and licked up her slit. Her head fell back as her nerve ends danced with delight. His tongue swirled around her clit, applying pressure and alternating between fast and slow. It drove her to the edge of climax, and then he slowed it all down again. He pushed a finger inside of her, following it with another. Both stretched out to ready her for his cock. Her head started to swim with all the sensations flooding her body —surreal and sensual, crazy and vibrant, all at the same time. She was swimming and drowning in happiness.

Pete pulled away from her and turned back to his trousers.

"What is it?"

"Condom."

"I'm on the pill. Bad periods when I was younger."

"I've never been so happy to hear that."

Pete came back over to her and settled his cock at her entrance. Miranda took in a deep breath and waited for him to push inside her. Instead of wondering what it was going to feel like for her, she imagined what he would be aware of in the intimacy of the coupling. But then a thought popped into her head –this was her first time but was it his?

"Wait." She stopped him as his hips drew back. He groaned but halted.

"What? Are you ok?" His eyebrows furrowed together, and he searched her face for signs of distress. She composed her features, though, to make sure none of her concerns showed at the thought she was given him her greatest gift, and this might not be his first time.

"Are you a virgin?" she blurted out.

"What?" he questioned with dumbfounded shock.

"Have you done this before?"

"I'm clean," he told her, and she recollected a disease her teachers had taught her about in sex education, which you caught during intercourse.

"That's not what I meant. You know, this is my first time. We've discussed it before, but I've never asked –will this be yours?"

Pete shut his eyes.

"As much as I want to play the big man and say I'm a pro at this sex thing, it's my first time also. I'm currently praying and pleading in my head that the second I put my cock inside you I'm able to make you feel something. I'm reciting banking terms in my head just to stop from coming too soon."

She leaned forward and brought his lips against hers.

"Account holder...compound interest...debt-to-income ratio," she teased.

"Fuck! When you say it, it's the sexiest thing I've ever heard."

Pete looked down at his cock sitting just outside her entrance and then back at her. He was asking for permission.

"Yes," she whispered, and he thrust slowly in until he

was fully seated to his hilt.

She felt the barrier to her virginity break and, despite the momentary pain, rejoiced at the fact they were finally as one. He gave her a moment to settle to the feeling of him, and she needed it for the overwhelming sense of fullness was threatening to engulf her in a powerful climax. Pete pulled his hips back and speared back into her. The sounds of their slick bodies moving together filled the room. Her soft moans of delight and his grunts of need echoed in her mind. It was a sound that would stay with her forever. Her first time and it was beautiful because it was with the man she would devote the rest of her life to loving.

Pete moved faster and faster, and the sensations inside her coiled tighter than a spring. Every part of her tingled with the awareness of her pleasure. A fire surged through her body and straight to the bunch of nerves between her thighs.

"Come," he ordered, and she complied. Her body convulsed against the powerful climax. Pete stilled, and his cock pulsed his own release deep into her body. The warm spurts mixing with her own essence to create a unity from the pleasures they'd taken.

When the stars stopped flying around her head, she registered Pete had collapsed onto the bed beside her. He'd withdrawn from her, and her tender flesh ached pleasantly.

"Wait here." He kissed the tip of her nose and rolled off the bed. She watched his pert backside as he strode confidently, but with a hint of exhaustion, into her ensuite bathroom. There was a rustling, and then she heard the turning on of taps followed by the sound of running water. That ceased, and he reappeared with a damp towel. He pressed it to her pussy, while she lay collapsed like a beached whale on the bed. Her legs were still there, but she was incapable of feeling them just yet. He cleaned her up and pulled the covers down, so she could nestle into her bed. He looked towards the door. She'd had a lock on it since she turned fifteen. It was something her mother had insisted on for her although she wasn't sure why. She should have thought about it before they'd had sex, but she'd been so caught in the moment she'd forgotten. She nodded at him to lock it. He obliged and came back into the bed next to her.

"You may need to take some paracetamol tomorrow because you'll probably feel sore. As much as I want to do that again and again tonight, we have a lifetime ahead, and I'm not going to damage you on the first night." A naughty grin spread across his face, and he pulled her into his arms.

"Stay," she begged.

"Until you fall asleep."

"I wish you could be here when I wake up." Her eyelids fluttered shut as exhaustion took over her body.

"I know. It won't always be this way." Pete kissed the top of her head, and she snuggled further into the warmth of his skin.

"I want to tell my father about us," she murmured half awake and half asleep. Before the darkness claimed her, she was sure she heard him reply.

"Not yet. I don't think I'll survive losing you."

CHAPTER SIX

Miranda

Miranda was dreading returning to Cambridge for her studies. She'd wanted to look at advancing further in English Literature and Art, but her father had insisted she do Economics and Mathematics, instead. She was good at those subjects, but they weren't her favourites. She would have no choice, though, if she hoped to avoid talk of her being married off to further her father's future ambitions. He'd mentioned it a few more times over the summer holidays and had even taken her to a social function where she's been introduced to several different men. She'd hated being there the entire time. None of the men spoke to her the way Pete did. She knew she'd lost her heart to the man she'd given her virginity to. With his commitments to his new job, and her father's ability to watch her like a hawk even though he had little interest in her, they had spent as much time as possible together over the summer.

One of the most exhilarating times they'd spent together was when Pete had showed her the new Ford Cortina he'd bought with his savings. It would enable him to drive up to meet her in Cambridge for weekends when she was away studying. They'd driven out to Broadstairs and had christened the back seat of the car numerous times before they returned home. She loved the car and had named it 'Cindy'. Pete hadn't been overly impressed with the name. He felt his car was more masculine than feminine and should have a boy's name, but she was adamant the car was a girl. She asserted it was the only other female that he would be allowed to ride, ever.

Miranda looked down at her watch. Pete was late. It was a Saturday morning, and the last before she had to return to college tomorrow. They were going to spend the day to-gether. She'd not been feeling at all well the last few days. A stomach bug had twisted her stomach and left her feeling exhausted and dizzy, but she wanted to enjoy the carefree time she had left. Her father had been away for the last week but was due to return later in the evening, so he could spend 'time' with her before she left. She wasn't sure why he bothered. He hadn't spent any time with her in the last sixteen years, so one night wouldn't make any difference. She'd rather spend the night with Pete buried deeply inside her. She giggled and covered her amusement with a hand over her mouth. She was turning into a bit of a sex fiend. She couldn't get enough.

A rap came from the window, and she jumped off her bed and sped across her room to open it.

"Hey, beautiful." Pete smirked with a playful raise of his eyebrow.

"Hey yourself." She licked her lips in anticipation of him finally climbing through the window and ravaging her. She'd been fantasying about it since she woke up this morn-ing.

"How are you feeling?" Pete asked and gently brought her into his arms, kissing her slowly. His tongue darted out and ran across the seam of her lips before delving in, tan-gling with hers in a passionate greeting.

"A lot better. I haven't been sick so far today, but break-fast was a boring affair of a slice of plain toast because I couldn't really stomach anything else."

"Are you sure you shouldn't see a doctor?" Pete frowned, and she pressed her lips against his, again, to reas-sure him she was fine and all that afflicted her was a stomach bug.

"I'm fine. I promise. It's probably nerves at having to go back to school. I don't want to leave you, I'm having so much fun." She pouted and pulled him to sit with her on the bed.

"If it continues, you have to promise me you'll go to the

doctor straight away."

"I promise." She leaned in to kiss him and then pulled back with a smile. "So, what are we doing today? Are we going out in Cindy?"

Pete groaned.

"I'm never going to be able to think of my car as anything but Cindy, now. You've damaged me." He ran his hand through his hair. The top part was getting a little long since he chose to spend all his free time with her rather than at a barber.

"Cindy is beautiful. It's a perfect name for your car."

He shook his head.

"Come on." Pete stood and held his hand out to her. She took it, and he led her back to the window and down the tree that he'd climbed up to reach her bedroom. Mr Pearson appeared from his workshop, overlooking her room and nodded at them. Pete waved back.

The chauffeur came over to them.

"I'm collecting your father at five pm. Make sure you're back and ready for dinner. He'll want it straight away as he has another meeting at eight pm."

She huffed. So much for spending the last evening with her father. Three hours was all she got. Most of that would be spent sitting in silence, eating a meal that no doubt would be his favourite and not hers, regardless of what her mother had promised. Lady Braybrooke was overridden at every stage of her endeavours to make her daughter's life better.

"I'll make sure she's back well before five." Pete pulled her hand up to his chest and held it by his heart. Mr Pearson nodded his acceptance.

"Drive carefully," the chauffeur warned.

"It's ok. We aren't going far. I've got some roller skates in the car, and we're going to go to the local park and have some fun."

"Now, I'm more worried"–Mr Pearson shuddered– "those things are death traps. Humans weren't intended to have wheels attached to their feet. No. Solid ground is best for me. If I want to do some spinning, I'll grab myself a dolly bird and head to the ballroom for a spot of foxtrotting." Miranda tried not to laugh when Mr Pearson held his arms up in a perfect hold position and wiggled off back to his workshop in a series of foxtrot promenade steps, mixed in with a couple of quickstep chassés

"He's insane." Pete chuckled quietly while leading her to his car, which he'd hidden off her father's land in the forest area surrounding the grounds.

"He is, but I wouldn't change him for anything. I miss him when I'm away from Braybrooke Hall. It's boring not having anyone to make me laugh." She went quiet and shuffled her feet on the summer sun-dried earth."

"Are you really nervous about going back?"

Pete leaned her against the car and stroked his hand down her cheek.

"I'm going to miss you. There's a big part of me that doesn't want to go. I want to stay locked here in this moment, but I know if I stay here, my father will forge ahead with his plans for my future. I will lose all control over what I want. I need to go back to school and get some qualifications, which will hold me in good stead when I walk away from here."

"It will be tight, but I can support you, if you want to walk away now."

She shook her head.

"No. I need to do this for myself as well. I don't want to be the stay at home woman. I want to do something with my life."

"You're doing something just by taking a chance. There are so many people out there who don't even do that." He brought himself closer to her and pinned her tenderly against the car.

"I want to be able to turn around and tell him I don't need him. That I've found my own way in life, and he needs to accept it. I've dreamt so many times of how I would do it, but I know the reality won't be anything like the fantasy."

She inhaled deeply and wiped away the tears that were forming in her eyes. She was so emotional lately. It was the thought of all the change.

"You'll try, won't you?" she uttered almost silently.

"Try?" Pete questioned.

"Us. Try to continue what we have. Try to come and see me?"

Pete pulled her closer into his arms and nestled her head against his heart.

"Miranda. I'll be with you whenever I can. I would walk away from everything here in London and find a job in Cambridge tomorrow if you gave me the word. I've told you. This is fate. You're mine. We may be kept apart for a little while longer, but we've found each other twice now, we can't be separated. I'll wait for you. I'll fight for you. I'll be yours, forever. This..." –he moved her back and placed his hand over his heart– "beats only for you. I want you. I love you. Never doubt what's in here."

"I love you." she whimpered back at him. "Damn." She looked up at the sky and silently cursed the fact she was all over the place today. "I'm a wreck. I'm sorry."

"Never apologise. I'll call you on that brick of a phone everyday if I can't get to Cambridge to see you. I'll be there every weekend without fail. Say the word, and I'll drop everything. I was going to do this later, but....."

Pete let go of her and dropped to his knee. He reached inside his jacket pocket and pulled out a small box. He opened it to reveal an engagement ring. She gasped and started to shake all over. Was this a dream? Was it really happening?

"It's not a proper diamond, yet, but it will be in the future. The car kind of wiped me out, but I needed it to get to see you. Miranda Braybrooke, I first set eyes on you eleven years ago, and I've not wanted anyone else since. Will you marry me?"

Tears now streamed down her cheeks. Words tried to

form in her mouth to answer him, but the emotions overwhelming her prevented anything that would sound remotely intelligent from coming out. Instead, she nodded her head, and then as common-sense came flooding back to her she cried,

"Yes, yes, yes." Pete pushed the ring onto her finger, and then standing back up, he brought her into his arms and twirled her around while kissing her.

"I love you!" he shouted.

"I love you, too," she repeated after him, and he sat her down on the ground. Bile suddenly flooded into her mouth, and her head started to spin violently. Before she knew what was happening, the ground was coming up to meet her, and her world turned black.

"Miranda?" The familiar gentle feminine voice pulled her back from the blackness. "Miranda, can you hear me?"

"Miranda?" That was Pete's voice, and it was laced with fear and trepidation. "We need to call a doctor?"

Her eyes sprang open. If they did, her father would be told she was unwell and that would lead to so many questions and the possible discovery of her relationship with the man currently holding her hand.

"Mum?" The form of the other voice in the room stood over her, holding a cold compress to her forehead.

"It's alright, my darling. You fainted, and Mr North brought you back." She looked around and realised she was lying on her own bed in her bedroom. "He said you hadn't been well. Why didn't you tell me? I knew you weren't eating as much as normal and seemed so tired." Her mother pulled the compress away from her forehead and held the back of her hand to Miranda's cheeks. You aren't hot, but you still look a little flushed. When was the last time you were sick?"

"Yesterday," she answered, and Pete squeezed her hand

tighter.

"Have you eaten today?" Her mother continued her questioning.

"I had a slice of toast a few hours ago."

"It could be the lack of food from previous days." Her mother's complexion turned paler. "I need to ask you some questions before we decide whether we need to call the doctor or not." Miranda watched as her mother stood away from the bed. It was then she noticed Mr Pearson stood in the room as well. Lines of worry etched onto his face.

"Mr North, it might be better if you let me have a few moments with my daughter."

Miranda shook her head fervently and held tighter to Pete's hand. She didn't want him going anywhere.

"It would seem she wishes me to stay with her if that is alright, Lady Braybrooke?"

Her mother lowered her head in acceptance and went over to Mr Pearson and whispered something into his ear. His eyes went wide, and he scurried from the room.

"Mother?" Miranda exclaimed. Her own feeling of trepidation rising with each passing moment.

"Sorry, darling." Her mother came back to the bed and took her other hand. "How long has your relationship with Mr North been going on? I see the ring on your finger." Her mother's head flicked to where the engagement ring was glistening on her left hand.

"Since June."

"Not long."

"We're soulmates, Lady Braybrooke," Pete interjected.

"I see it in the worry showing on your face, Mr North. Please don't fear my reaction on that score. I'm not my husband. I suspected my daughter was seeing someone. You should have told me, darling."

"I'm sorry, Mother. I didn't want to put you in a position where you would need to lie to father."

"I can handle him myself." Her mother stumbled over the words and ran a finger over the back of Miranda's hand.

"Is your relationship physical? Erm...intimate."

"Sexual?" Pete offered, and Miranda felt her cheeks flush bright red.

"Yes." Her mother turned a pinker shade herself. Miranda had never learned about relationships from her parents. It wasn't the done thing amongst the upper classes. Not when school could provide the full details and not just the brief outline an embarrassed person would.

"Yes. Our relationship is sexual and has been for a few months, now."

Miranda's stomach lurched again. She let go of both hands holding hers and brought her hands up to her mouth as the knowledge of what could be wrong with her dawned. She frantically tried to remember when her last period had been but kept coming back to the same answer: when she'd finished school for the summer. She hadn't had one since then.

"Do you need the sick bowl?" Pete held up a bucket. She could tell by the look on his face he was more concerned about her vomiting again than contemplating the reason behind her current bout of sickness.

Mr Pearson chose that moment to rush back into the room with a box under his arm. He handed it to her mother, and Miranda knew instantly what it was. Her mother twisted the box around in her hand and checked a date on it.

"Still in date."

"No," Miranda lamented.

"Miranda?" Pete pulled her closely. "What is it?"

"You need to take it, my darling. We need to be certain before we tell him."

"No. He can't know. He can't know, ever."

"What?" Pete grabbed the box out of her mother's hand in frustration. His face went white as a sheet as he realised he held a pregnancy test in his hand. "You're on the pill, though? We didn't use a condom."

"You had the stomach bug just after you returned from school. If you'd vomited the pill, then you could have lost protection."

Miranda felt her head starting to spin again with every-thing she was trying to take in.

Pete dropped the test on the bed and pulled her closer.

"It's ok. We just got engaged. I wasn't expecting a baby straight away, but if the test is positive, then we'll just be a family sooner rather than later."

"I'm not seventeen, yet," she mumbled almost incoher-ently.

"Doesn't matter," Pete reassured her.

"You need to take the test, my darling," her mother urged, again.

Miranda looked to where Mr Pearson stood on the balls of his feet. His hands were clasped together in front of him. He looked older than she thought he'd ever looked before. She'd done that to him. He adored her more than her father ever would, and her situation was causing him worry.

She picked the test up and slid from the bed. Pete helped her walk on wobbly legs to the bathroom. He made to enter with her, but she pushed him away.

"We do this together. I'm staying with you."

"But I've got to...." she whispered and looked towards her mother.

"Pee into a bottle. I know. Still going nowhere. When we're living together, finally, we'll have no shut doors be-tween us."

"Ok."

They both entered the bathroom, and Pete shut the door behind them. He took the box from her hand, opened it up, and handed her the container.

"It says you need to wee into this." He pointed to the contraption in her hand. "Then, we have to wait."

"Will you at least turn around while I do the first bit? It feels strange."

He nodded and turned his back to her. Miranda placed the container on the sink and pulled down her jeans and panties. She retrieved the container and placed it under her while hovering over the toilet. She did her business and placed the container back on the sink while she flushed the toilet. She followed the instructions on the test packaging and then washed her hands.

Pete turned around when he heard the toilet go and brought her into his arms. Her mind was reeling. She wasn't sure how long she'd been unconsciousness, so time was a bit fluffy, but no more than half an hour ago they had been discussing a future that was nothing like this. If she were pregnant, she wouldn't be able to go back to school. It wouldn't change her plans to marry Pete, however, it would mean it'd probably happen a bit earlier than they'd expected. She and Pete could have created a small human, and it may be growing inside her. The thought warmed her, and she slid a hand across her belly to rest it there. Pete brought his to rest on hers.

"I'm not going anywhere, no matter what that says."

"I know." She leaned back into him, and he kissed her neck. "We should go back outside. My mother will want to know straight away. She will need to prepare for what we'll tell my father."

"She won't have to tell him anything. I will." Pete picked up the test from the sink, and she winced a little. He was touching the test containing her pee, but it didn't seem to bother him in the slightest.

When enough time had passed, he held the test up and looked at it and then to the instructions. He exhaled deeply and handed it to her. She didn't need the instructions, though, to tell from the result staring back at her: she was pregnant.

CHAPTER SEVEN

Pete

Pete slipped out of the room and left Miranda sobbing into her mother's lap from the shock and fear of what would happen next. Her father's impending reaction weighed heavily on them all. He needed a few minutes to collect his thoughts. He was going to be a father and a lot sooner than he thought it would happen. Strangely, though, he wasn't scared. He knew Miranda would make a perfect mother. He'd try his hardest to be a great father, and if he followed his own father's example, then he'd do alright. The door closed behind him, and Mr Pearson filled the corridor.

"Is this where you hit me for getting her into trouble?" he asked.

"It takes two to tango. I can see you love that girl and won't be going anywhere."

"I'm not. Even on my death bed, she'll be my first, last, and only thought."

"You know her father's going to try and implement the death bit." Mr Pearson raised a telling eyebrow at him.

"I don't doubt it at all. I just have to hope I made so little of an impression on him at the bank that he forgets I'm just a trainee."

"That, or you discover in the next few hours you're some rich and titled gentleman. That would probably be the best thing you could do."

"Yes. But I don't think it's going to happen. Ken and Elise North aren't really the gentry type. Not when my father was born in the East End."

"I was hoping it would be at least Kensington way."

"Sorry."

Pete shrugged his shoulders.

"I wish I could give you some indication on how Lord Braybrooke is going to take the news, but I've got no idea. He likes to play games and to win them, having only a daughter is the biggest loss to him. She's a pawn in his aspirations. He won't take this lying down. You need to be ready to fight for her and the child. It'll get hard, but you'll have my support as much as I can give."

"Thank you. Your vote of confidence means a lot. I won't let her down."

Mr Pearson held his hand out. Pete took it and shook it. The older man then ran his hand over his brow. "It's time for me to go and get him. Prepare what you're going to say. I'll be back in half an hour."

"Good luck with that. Try and keep him in a good mood."

Mr Pearson let out a belly laugh.

"I don't think good mood and Lord Braybrooke have ever been used in the same sentence before. You are a great joker."

Pete gulped.

Mr Pearson reached into his large pocket and pulled out a mobile phone.

"I was going to give this to you when she went back to school, but I think you need it now." He handed him the phone. "It's a spare. He never looks at the bills anyway, so you've got it if you need to call her and can't be with her. Her father never lets her leave her phone behind."

Pete took the phone and looked down at it in shock and confusion.

"You don't have to."

"Take it. I really need to go." The chauffeur hurried down the corridor. Pete looked at the phone in his hand. The urgency he felt in his bones to speak to one particular person overruled his need to return to Miranda. He punched the numbers he'd memorised into the device and pressed call. The phone crackled into life, and the digital ringtones echoed into his ear.

"Hello?" His mother's voice came on the other end, and he sighed in relief. It worked.

"Hi, Mum."

"Pete. Are you ok? I thought you were doing extra work all day?" He heard the clatter of dishes in the background, and he knew his mother was cooking up a feast again for their dinner. Saturday night was always fish and chips night, followed by one of her cakes covered in glazed fruits.

"Is Dad there?"

"Of course. I think he's checking the football scores. Hang on." The phone went muffled, and he heard his mother shouting out 'Ken'. There was more rustling, and after a few minutes, his father's voice came on the other end of the line.

"Hey, kiddo. You ok?" Despite the fact he was eighteen, his father still called him kiddo. It was a nickname that'd always stuck.

"Hi, Dad. Do you remember the summer we went to Broadstairs and I gave that little girl my ice-cream after she lost hers?"

"Your first love. How can I forget?" His father laughed.

"I've asked her to marry me."

"What?" His father sounded confused, but given he probably wasn't making much sense, Pete wasn't surprised. He'd told his parents he'd met someone but nothing else.

"I found her again. She's the girl I've been dating. Dad, we had an accident. She's pregnant."

He heard his mother gasp and surmised she must have been listening into the conversation as well.

"Well it's too late for me to tell you to be careful." There was a hint of anger in his father's voice, but Pete knew he was trying to mask it because of the love and support he always got from his parents. "How is she?"

"Feeling sick. She fainted. Dad, we may need somewhere to stay. Her father, he's not a good man. He's nobility and treats her like dirt. We're going to tell him later, but I think he may abandon her. I love her, Dad, and I want to be with her forever."

The line went silent for a few moments. His father was thinking.

"Dad?"

"Elsie, go change the sheets on Pete's bed. I'll start tidying up his room. We'll make some space in the wardrobe for her to put her stuff in. It'll be alright son. You love her. That's all you'll need."

"Thank you." He felt the lump forming in his throat. "I better get back to her."

"We'll be here when you come home."

Pete finished the call and put the phone away. He took a few more moments to compose himself and re-entered Miranda's bedroom. She was standing in front of a full-length mirror looking at her sideways reflection.

"I think I can see a little bump already." Miranda stroked her completely flat belly. Her mother smirked at him and mouthed,

"Is everything alright?"

He nodded at her and went over to Miranda.

"Mr Pearson has gone to get your father. I think you should pack a little bag of essentials just in case."

Miranda's eye's widened, and she looked over at her mother who nodded in agreement.

"Nobody knows what his reaction will be. All we can do is wait."

It was the longest half an hour of Pete's life. Numerous different outcomes had run through his head by the time the wheels of the returning car kicked up the gravel on the driveway. Lord Braybrooke's stern voice came up the stairs in a bellow for his wife and child to join him for dinner. Augusta got to her feet and straightened the long dress she was wearing. The matching pearl earrings looked far too big for her ears, but Pete knew it was the fashion. Miranda had gone so white she looked like a ghost.

"I think I might be sick." She held her hands over her mouth, and Pete rushed to her side with the bucket again.

She dry heaved over it a few times before deciding she'd be alright

Lord Braybrooke's voice came up the stairs again, this time with more anger in it.

"We need to go now before he gets too angry." Miranda grabbed his hand and dragged him towards the door. She stopped at the threshold and kissed him. "I love you."

"I love you, too," he replied without hesitation and opened the door for her to go through. They were instantly met with the imposing figure of her father and a pale Mr Pearson standing behind him.

"What the hell is going on?" Time seemed to stand still as her father spoke. Venom laced each of his words with a stinging bite.

"Daddy, I'd like to introduce you to Peter North." Miranda held herself up tall and didn't seem to allow the big man to intimidate her. Pete knew differently, though, from the shaking of her hand.

"Why was he in your bedroom?"

Miranda's mother appeared behind them, and her father's eyes almost stood out on stalks with the shock.

"Augusta?"

"Please listen to them, Charles. What they have to say is important."

Pete cleared his throat and stepped forward.

"Lord Braybrooke, it's a pleasure to finally meet you." Pete held his hand out, but Miranda's father only looked at it like it was covered in dog shit. "Miranda and I have something we wish to tell you. I asked her to marry me earlier, and she said yes."

Her father burst out into a fit of laughter. It wasn't exactly the response Pete was expecting. In fact it hadn't figured in any of the scenarios he'd imagined over the last thirty minutes.

"Mr Pearson, would you escort this vagabond out of my house? If he thinks he can come here and make stupid promises to my daughter, then he has another think coming. I'm not a fool. Give him some money to make him go away...permanently. I'm sure that is all he wants."

"I'm pregnant," Miranda blurted out. "He's the father, and he's not going anywhere.

Flames of fury licked up the sides of Lord Braybrooke's cheeks, and Pete was certain that if it were possible he would be seeing steam coming out of the ears of the man in front of him, right now.

"Pregnant?" her father repeated.

"Yes."

Without another response, her father turned on his heels and stomped off down the stairs. Miranda looked to her mother.

"Is that it?"

She shook her head.

"You need to follow him."

Solemnly, they followed down the stairs towards the sound of Miranda's father. He was on the phone. "I need you here, now."

Silence.

They walked into the lounge to find him pouring himself a brandy from an ornate decanter perched upon a dark mahogany dresser.

"Do you realise what you've done?" He spoke into the amber nectar and not directly at them.

"Daddy, please." Miranda stepped forward, and Pete let her go. He was on hand should he be needed to protect her, but this wasn't a battle he could fight for her. It was one she needed to win herself. "I fell in love. Please, this is a happy accident."

"You're sixteen." Her father spun around to face Miranda. His eyes were black as the night with the anger coursing through his veins.

"Age is nothing but a number when it comes to what I feel. Pete is a good man. He's intelligent and... and... I know you're worried about the future of our family name, but he'll be a good asset for it."

"You actually think I'll allow him to inherit after me. A kid who has fooled around with my daughter and got her in the family way." Lord Braybrooke turned his malevolent focus back to Pete. "Who are you? What is your pedigree? Your parents? Your finances. Tell me?"

Pete had been right. Their meeting in the bank was so insignificant to Miranda's father he'd forgotten him.

"My name is Peter North; my parents are Ken and Elsie. I have some money and a good job. My prospects for a superior position are good. I can get references should you wish. I can and will look after your daughter." He dared to take a step closer. "I'm not stupid, Lord Braybrooke. I know the situation we find ourselves in is not ideal at our age, but I want to care for you daughter and marry her. I'll do it with or without your blessing, but we really would prefer with."

There was the bark of laughter again.

"You think I'll allow this marriage to happen?" The doors behind them flew open and two heavy set men thundered in with fists clenched.

"Daddy, no." Miranda reached out to grab her father, but he pushed her away.

"You disgust me. You've always been a selfish little brat. I thought for once you might think of someone other than yourself and accept the man I chose to be your husband, But I can see you've opened your legs for the first person who's shown any interest in you."

"That's not true," Miranda countered. "I love him."

"You love the idea of affection."

"Well, is it any wonder given I've been starved of it most of my life?" Miranda slapped her hands over her mouth, realising at the last minute that what she was saying would antagonise her father further.

The two men bore down on Pete with fists smacking against open palms. This was about to get painful, very painful, judging by the men's expressions. Miranda's mother and Mr Pearson entered the room.

"Charles, please listen to them. This isn't some sordid

encounter. This is emotional."

"You knew?" her father bellowed, and it felt like the whole room shook.

"I only found out today, but I've seen the affection Mr North has for our daughter. He truly loves her. I'm sure we can sort something out. You could educate Mr North on what you need for a successor. He could be a powerful future holder of the name with your guidance. I'm sure he'd even consent to taking the name Braybrooke for Miranda's sake if you asked?" Pete knew Augusta Braybrooke was trying to play to her husband's weaknesses to make him see sense, but the look of disgust on his face told him it wasn't working.

Determination spread across Lord Braybrooke's face, and it sent shivers down Pete's spine. The devil himself was in front of them and about to wreak havoc.

"You two"–he pointed to the burly men who now stood either side of him– "deal with him." One of the men grabbed him, and the other sent a stomach crunching punch into his torso. He gasped out in agony.

"Daddy." Miranda ran to get in the way, but she wasn't quick enough. Her father grabbed her by the hair and pulled her in closely to him. She screamed, and it scared Pete enough to try and break free of the men. He wasn't strong enough, though, and another blow came, this time breaking his nose and shooting blood all over the floor.

"No!" Miranda screamed again.

"You slut," her father screeched. "You've destroyed everything. How can I ever sell you for a virgin, now, when you have this insignificant's spawn inside you? I should beat you black and blue until you lose the foetus, but I won't be responsible for taking the life of your mistake. No, you'll have to live with what you've done forever."

Pete tried his hardest to keep focused on what was being said to Miranda. Was he casting her out of the family? The beating would be worth it if Miranda would be free to live her life.

"Mr Pearson?"

The chauffeur stepped forward.

"Take Miranda and put her in the car."

"Sir?" He stepped forward tentatively. "What then, Sir?"

"We'll take her somewhere this lowlife can never find her. She'll have her brat, and then I'll give it away, so she can never see it again. Afterwards she'll be married off and bedded as the whore she is, but this time at my whim."

"Sir." Mr Pearson hesitated.

"Charles." Augusta Braybrooke came up to her husband and got down on her knees in front of him to beg. "Please, don't do this."

The Lord's large hand came out, and he slapped it hard across his wife's face. She tumbled onto the floor, her head hitting the side of a table. Her body lay limp.

"Mummy." Miranda, who was still being held by her father, was hysterical by this point.

"Shut up." Her father shook her. "Get her in the car," Lord Braybrooke ordered the chauffeur again just as another punch sent Pete down onto his knees. His world was starting to blur at the edges, but he needed to remain focused.

"No." Mr Pearson stepped forward and used as much of his dwindling from old age bulk to intimidate his employer.

"You've been helping them." Realisation dawned on the Lord's face.

"They're in love."

"Get out," Lord Braybrooke ordered.

"Not without Miranda, Pete, and Lady Augusta. I won't watch you destroy their lives, any longer, with your greed and envy." From his slumped position on the floor, Pete was proud of the way the chauffeur was standing up for them. Miranda had pulled her mother towards her. The Lady appeared to be dizzy and disoriented but was moving, albeit slowly. A shadow walked in front of him, and before Pete could open his mouth to warn Mr Pearson, one of the two brutes who had been attacking him sent a vase smashing over the driver's head. He collapsed to more screaming from Miranda.

Lord Braybrooke gritted his teeth and snarled at the same time, grabbing Miranda and pulling her to her feet.

"Finish them. Leave my wife for me to deal with."
Pete tried his hardest to stand up, to fight back, but he was too weakened. All he could do was look on as Miranda was dragged from the room by her father.

"Miranda!" he shouted after her and received nothing back but her frantic cries for help. He went down on his hands and knees, crawling towards the door. He knew he wouldn't make it through when he felt the debilitating pain of something shattering the bones in his leg. The darkness claimed him, and Miranda was gone.

CHAPTER EIGHT

Miranda

Days of loneliness and captivity turned into months, and the entire time Miranda's abdomen swelled with the child growing inside. Occasionally, a midwife would come and check on her but apart from that, she saw no one. Her food was delivered by the same mute servant who never even raised her eyes from the floor to look at her. She had no idea where she was or how long she'd been there, but the fact the baby within her blocked all view of her feet and its head was engaged, according to the last midwife visit, indicated she was near to full term. The baby would be born and taken from her. She'd no idea if Pete was even alive. If he were, had he given up on her? The tears fell as she tried to get comfortable on the run-down bed, which was the only piece of furniture in the primitive dungeon she lived in.

Her father had visited a few times, and the contempt and disgust she felt for him had grown each time. The way he'd spoken down to her had extinguished any hope she'd held for him having any goodness in him. He was an evil man and cared for only himself. He hid behind the pretence of making decisions for the future good of the title, but he couldn't really care less about that. It was purely selfish, and she knew when this was over she would be sold to the highest bidder as a trophy wife. Money –everything was about that. Her father wanted as much as he could get for himself. He wanted prestige and to own the greatest name in the country. At least by marrying, Miranda would lose the name Braybrooke and never have to use it again. She couldn't wait.

It was impossible to get comfortable. Her back had been aching all afternoon, and all she wanted to do was curl up into a little ball and sleep through the rest of her life.

She looked up when the door opened. Her father stomped in with the midwife behind him.

"Get up," he ordered her. There was still an edge of defiance in her, which grew every day, so she ignored him. "I said get up," he repeated louder and with more venom.

She rolled over, so she didn't have to face them. Next thing she knew, she was being pulled from the bed and flung across the room.

"Lord Braybrooke, please, the child." The midwife came to her side to check on her, but Miranda slapped her away and protectively cradled her arm around her stomach.

"I couldn't give a fuck about that thing inside her. I want it out, now. So, get it out!"

"I really don't think this is a good idea." The midwife tried to comfort her again, but Miranda just stared daggers at her.

"You said she was thirty-eight weeks, meaning the baby will live if it's born. Now, do what I pay you to do."

"Don't touch me!" she screamed.

"Oh, for crying out loud." Her father came over and pulled her to her feet. She was helpless with her size and lack of strength, compared to him. He dragged her out of the room and along a dark corridor she vaguely remembered from when she was brought here. She tried to quickly do the maths in her head. She'd have been roughly six weeks pregnant when she arrived. That would've been thirty-two weeks ago. She choked out a garbled cry for Pete. It'd been so long. It would be March now. She'd missed the autumn and winter while hidden away. Her father stopped and slammed her against the wall. She whimpered with pain.

"He's gone. You'll never see him again. Get used to it, you little whore. We're going to get this bastard out of you, and then I'll deal with you, just as you deserve. You'll spend the rest of your life flat on your back. I've got just the husband for you, and he isn't bothered by the fact you're not a virgin. It tells him just what sort of woman you are. You think I'm the devil? Well, I've got nothing on him. His relatives are notorious in society, especially his cousin the Duke of Oakfield." Her father pulled her away from the wall and resumed hauling her towards another room. He kicked the door open as he approached, and several of the people inside, who were dressed in medical scrubs, jumped back. The room was white and clinical. There was a bed in the middle of it.

"Your patient," her father snarled and thrust her towards them. She tried to turn and run before she was caught, but being heavily pregnant left her incapable of fast movement. One of the men caught her and sneered. She noticed beneath the face mask it was one of the men who'd been in the room that fateful day when she'd told her father what was happening. She raised her hand to slap him for what he'd done to Pete. For all she knew this man was her lover's murderer. He caught her tiny wrist, though, and flipped her around to bend over the table and pulled up her top.

"Doctor," he ordered, and a timid man stepped forward. "The epidural."

Miranda knew in an instant what was happening. The knives on the table in front of her gleamed brightly in the clinical light. They were going to cut her baby from her.

"No." She tried her hardest to struggle, but the weight of the man behind her prevented any movement. The doctor disappeared from her vision, and she cried out when a sharp pain shot through her lower back. A cold liquid flooded into her body, and she was pulled up onto the table and held down.

"How long?" her father asked.

"The drugs should work in about ten to twenty minutes and up to another forty minutes for the baby to be born," the doctor replied.

"I'll be back in forty-five. You better have it out by then," her father responded and went for the door.

"Daddy, please," Miranda called out.

Her father turned.

"Please, don't do this. Please. Let me go. I'll disappear. You can choose whoever you want to give the title to. My uncle can't dispute it if I lie. Say that the person is your son. I'm sure if you can do all of this, then you can hire someone to falsify a DNA test. Please. Let me go. I'm your daughter."

Her father threw back his head and laughed. Miranda blinked back the tears in her eyes.

"Finally, you show there's a bit of me in you and not just the soppy neediness of your mother. She'll be so pleased to know that." Confirmation her mother was still alive slammed into her with the realisation that possibly the same could be said for Pete. Maybe he was out there looking for her. She just needed to hang on. "Too little too late, though." Her father turned heel and walked back out, slamming the door behind him.

"No!" she screamed and tried to pull away from the man holding her down. She scratched at him and bit down on his arm. He had no choice other than to let her go, but as she slid from the bed, the drugs coursing through her body started to work and her legs went from under her. The feeling in them gone. "No!" she cried as she was unceremoniously picked up and dropped back on the bed. The man she'd bitten, seething at having a chunk taken out of his arm, took great delight in removing the clothing from the lower half of her body.

"Do it now!"

he ordered, and the doctor went white.

"I can't. The drugs haven't fully spread through her system."

"I don't care." Her father's hired thug picked up one of the surgical knives and handed it to the doctor. "Now, or I'll be using that on you."

Another man came to her feet and held them down while the man who'd ordered her torture placed both his hands on her shoulders and stared down into her eyes from his vantage point at her head.

"We need to cover her lower half from view." The mid-wife stepped up with a cloth and stammered out her nervous words. Miranda didn't doubt they were being paid handsomely for what they were about to do, but professional ethics still weighed heavily on their minds. She looked up to the man looming over her. His facial expression told her no covering up would be done, and she would witness every sick and twisted element of what was about to happen to her.

The doctor stepped up and with a gulp pressed his hand on to her abdomen. Thankfully, the drugs had worked quickly, and the sensations around her midsection and legs were gone. She felt nothing. A tear dropped from her eye when the doctor looked at her and whispered, "Sorry.".

He pulled his hand back and made the first cut with the knife. Fortunately, the swell of her abdomen hid her view of everything. Seeing her insides would probably have caused her to be violently sick. She lay as still as she could. There was no point in struggling, now. She needed to help those who were about to rip her child from her belly. To deliver her baby safely, she needed to remain calm and quiet and allow them to do their work. Her impending motherhood washed over her with this new found eerie compose.

Before long, she heard the cry of a baby. Her breath caught in her throat as the new-born was delivered onto her chest. The man holding her let go of her arms, and she instantly brought the baby to her and held it tightly. It was perfect, beautiful, and a miracle all wrapped up in one tiny bundle. She looked down and saw it was a boy. Pete would have been so proud to have a son. She silenced the distraught cries of the infant with a 'coo' and kissed the top of his forehead.

The room around them had fallen silent except for the noises she and the baby made. His tiny lips moved, and his tongue darted out looking for food. She didn't care who was around and removed her breast from the bra she still wore.

The baby knew instantly where to find food and with a little bit of trouble latched on to her breast. It felt natural. Tears streamed down her face. She was vaguely aware of work continuing around her, the afterbirth being removed, the umbilical cord being clamped and cut, and stitches being put in place, but all her focus was on the baby.

"She shouldn't be feeding it." The man who she'd bitten spoke up, but the midwife pulled him away.

"The first milk is important."

"It's not an it." She spoke without diverting her attention from her son, "His name is Ryan. Ryan Peter North."

Miranda pulled her gaze away from the baby for a moment when the door opened, and her father walked in. He looked from her to the baby.

"Is it ready?" he asked with zero emotion in his voice. This baby was his grandchild, but it could have been a dirty rag on the floor for all he cared. That sent shivers of fear through Miranda.

"Yes," the midwife spoke up.

"Bring it." Her father turned and left the room, again.

The midwife came up to Miranda with tears forming in her own eyes. "I'm sorry." Before Miranda could register what was going on, Ryan was removed from her chest, wrapped in a blanket, and taken towards the door. He started to scream for her, for her milk, for his mother. She tried to move, but the men were back and holding her down.

"No!" she screamed repeatedly. She was thrashing around on the bed trying her hardest to go after her child as he was carried from the room. "Ryan!!"

"She's going to do herself damage," the doctor shouted. "give me a sedative, now."

"No." She tried even harder to move, but the people around her were too quick, and the needle flooded the tranquillising fluid into her arm. As it took her body into oblivion, she knew she would never see her son again.

CHAPTER NINE

Pete

Another dead end.

Another false hope.

Another time when he would return home without Miranda and their child.

He looked up once more at the run-down castle in the Highlands of Scotland before getting in his car and heading back towards the cheapest bed and breakfast he'd been able to find.

Pete had done the calculations so often now. He knew Miranda was due any day or had probably already had their child, depending on how far along she was when they'd discovered her pregnancy. Eight months had gone by so quickly. Although given he'd spent half of it unconscious in a hospital bed, it wasn't surprising. His mother had sobbed by his bedside as his father explained he'd been found in the gutter outside Barratt's bank with a shattered leg, a broken jaw, and internal injuries so numerous his parents were told if they were religious, to call a priest for last rites. It was another three months before they'd allowed him out of the hospital because it had taken him that long to be able to walk again. His leg would cause trouble for the rest of life, but he hadn't lost it, which had been the initial fear.

As soon as he was strong enough, well maybe sooner than he should have, he quit his job and was out looking for Miranda. His first port of call had been to find Mr Pearson. The elderly chauffeur had been in the same hospital as him. Neither of them had spoken about their injuries to the police. As far as the authorities were concerned, they'd both been attacked by an unconnected mystery assailant for their wallets. He had, however, tried to report Miranda to the police as missing. But, it seemed money talked when it came to a person being recorded as unaccounted for, and his plea for help had fallen on deaf ears. It was up to him to find Miranda. Hopefully, before her father damaged her irrevocably if it were even possible at this late stage.

"I'm back," Pete called as he entered the accommodation in which they were both staying. Mr Pearson, or *Jim* as Pete had come to know the chauffeur, had taken longer to heal from his wounds. In fact, his arm was still in a sling from the fracture he'd received, and Jim's memory was poor at best, now, because of the impact of the vase against his skull.

"Did you find her?" Jim was out of his chair and expectant.

"No. It was another dead end."

"Damn it." The old man hit the side of the chair with his good hand. "We're running out of time."

"I know." Pete went over to the fridge in the corner of their room and pulled out a beer. He'd found himself drinking a lot more recently. It numbed the pain and help him sleep. March in Scotland was damp, and it did little to help the fragile bones in his leg. Then there were the thoughts constantly running through his mind concerning Miranda and what was happening to her. He flipped back the pull ring and took a long drink.

"We have that other lead. I'll try that tomorrow."

"It'll come to nothing." Jim sat back down in an armchair, his body hunched over in defeat. The old man thought of Miranda as his daughter. He cared for her in a way Miranda's own father never had.

Pete ambled over to Jim and put his hand on his shoulder.

"I promise you we'll find her. I won't stop until I do. I've found her twice now in my life. The third time will be forever."

A quiet knock at the door drew both their attentions.

"Were you followed?" Jim asked.

"No, I checked repeatedly."

"If he knows we're looking for her..."

Pete held his finger up to his mouth to silence Jim.

"Who is it?" he called out.

Silence.

He and Jim looked at each other, a bead of sweat developed on his brow.

Jim picked up a bat they'd brought with them, just in case. It had been resting in the corner of the room. He motioned for Pete to open the door. Reluctantly, Pete stepped forward. His mouth fell open when he saw who was on the other side.

"Lady Augusta."

Miranda's mother stood in front of him. A fur coat wrapped around her to guard against the chill in the air. She pushed past him and into the room.

"I'm sorry for my rudeness, but I don't have much time. I'd hoped and prayed you'd pull through, but your injuries....They were so severe. I know if I hadn't forced them to take me from the property by causing such a scene, they would have killed you both."

"Miranda?" Pete stepped up to her. His fists were clenched with the need for information. "Where is she?"

"That's what I'm here to tell you. She's been kept from me as well." Augusta burst into tears. "The baby, she's had it. They...they did a caesarean as soon as they could."

"I'm a Father?" Pete's ears started to ring with the blood whooshing around his head. "Where is it...er...he? She?"

"He, Ryan, she named him Ryan." Miranda's mother stumbled, and Jim was up and helping her into his chair.

"The beer." He waved towards the can he'd left on the desk.

Pete retrieved it and offered it to Augusta.

She took a sip and screwed her nose up in repulsion.

"Thank you. I'm sorry."

"Lady Augusta, where is my son?" He knelt in front of her.

"I don't know. My husband, he's always been insane, but the last few months even I don't recognise him. It's like he has become so consumed by everything he's lost all his humanity."

"What did he do to you?" Jim asked and placed his hands around Augusta's.

"Miranda. We need to focus on her."

"Augusta." Jim squeezed, and it was the first time Pete saw the fatherly care for Miranda also extended to her mother.

"He took his rights from me as my husband....violently. I'll heal just as you will. Miranda is the one I'm worried about. Pete."– Lady Augusta turned her attention from his roommate to stare directly at him– "she's to be married to a man who'll treat her even worse than her father. She's not strong, now, with the loss of her baby. I've tried to search my husband's records to find out what has happened to him, but there's nothing. He's disappeared off the face of the Earth, and although I know my husband won't kill him, you won't be able to find him. He'll have made certain of that."

"If he's alive, there's always hope, but I agree with you we need to get to Miranda. Where is she?"

"She's at a house outside Dumfries. It's a remote location. I saw her yesterday for the first time. She's very weak but capable of running should it be needed." She reached into the pocket of her coat and pulled out the address and another piece of paper.

"What's this?"

"It's notice of your intended marriage. You can marry in Gretna Green without parental consent. I placed the notice a week back when I was told this other marriage was to take place. Go to the address tonight and rescue her. Take her to Gretna and hide for the next few days, and then, you'll be able to marry. Find the Blacksmith."

"What?" Pete shook his head as confusion clouded his mind.

"Marrying her is the only way to stop this. Bind her to you and make her yours forever. It's the only way her father will give up. I've been looking through all his family history and the governing documents of his properties and titles. Only Miranda's first husband will be able to inherit. Should she divorce, then it's null and void, and the estate goes to my brother-in-law. She'd be completely useless to him and his aspirations. She'll be free."

"I'm not sure I can get my head around all of this." Pete rubbed his forehead. "Free. To live. The one thing she's wanted to do forever. To be herself and make decisions based on her own learning and hopes for the future."

"Yes. Free."

The room fell silent.

"What about you?" Jim knelt also. His old bones creaking.

Augusta reached out and stroked her hand down his face. This was a gesture that would've been intimate in so many situations, but in this instance, it was one of respect. "I lost my freedom the day I married Lord Braybrooke. My decisions have been made for me, and I'll live by them because it's all I know. This has been who I am for so long, now, I don't know any different. What's on the other side would destroy me. I wouldn't survive it." Her voice broke on the last word, despite her desperately trying to stop it from doing so. "Go save my little girl."

With those final words, Pete got to his feet, stepped back, and allowed Augusta to rise gracefully out of the chair. She adjusted her coat again, so it wrapped around her tiny frame as a barrier to the cold and the world. Within the protection of the fabric, she could be whoever she wanted to be and not just the downtrodden wife of a tyrant. Augusta bowed her head to them both and left them alone in the silent room.

The ticking of a clock reminded Pete time was passing. He had the address of where the woman he loved was, and he was standing here lamenting the fate of her mother.

Jim, who'd risen to his feet as a show of respect to Augusta when she left, bent and retrieved a briefcase from under his bed. He clicked the locks to open it and pulled out a gun. Pete's eyes went wide.

"Let's go." Jim pushed the pistol into the back of his trousers. "Don't fail me now, boy. When you've lived through a World War, handling one of these is nothing. Try facing down a grenade."

"I think it's just dawning on me what we're going to have to do to save her."

"Whatever we need to." Jim responded.

"Whatever we need to."

CHAPTER TEN

Miranda

It felt like a cold wind had swept over her body as Miranda looked into the mirror in front of her. The last time she looked at her reflection, she was imagining how she'd look with the child she'd conceived with Pete, heavy in her belly. The girl staring back at her this time had lost all of the excitement and spirit of that previous one. This one was broken beyond all repair. The baby was no longer there, cut out of her stomach and taken away after barely drawing his first breath. The hope for a future filled with love and devotion torn away by a man who was supposed to love her.

Her hand moved to the chain and locket around her neck. As much as she hated the midwife for what she'd helped do, she also respected her for her actions afterwards. She'd returned later that evening to check on Miranda and had brought a locket, containing hair from her son. She'd apologised and told her about her own children she never got to see. They'd been taken away from her because she couldn't afford to look after them. The job the midwife had just undertaken would allow her to get them back. A child for a child. Miranda hadn't thanked her. She'd simply taken the locket and placed it around her neck. That had been six weeks ago. Today, she'd been given the all clear after her caesarean and was to be married.

She'd met the man once when her father had brought him to where ever it was in the world she was staying. She wished she could say he was handsome or even a nice man, but he was neither. He was at least fifteen years older than her, and his physique was nothing in comparison to Pete's lean and toned muscular body. His eyes were beady, and they bore into her as though he was having lustful thoughts.

She'd ignored him at first, but that had only seemed to increase his feelings of inadequacy at having to buy a wife rather than have one fall in love with him. In front of her father, he'd punched her in the face for showing him disrespect. Her father hadn't cared, though, and sanctioned the action as necessary because of her insolence. The bright purple bruise surrounding her eye stood out against the paleness of her reflection. The white wedding gown she was forced to wear doing little to give her colour.

She turned away from her image. It was tormenting her even further, causing more problems in her already jumbled mind. With a long exhalation, she trudged over to the window and looked out. The world outside was blossoming with the signs of spring. Daffodils bloomed in yellow, flowers of hope for the coming year. She had none. She was more like the snowdrops that had withered and died, having blanketed the grass only a few short weeks ago with their splendour.

Pete must have died or given up on her. She'd still had no word from him. He'd not come when their baby had been taken, and he wouldn't come today. She was alone, broken, ashamed. No one truly loved her.

She wiped a tear away from her eye, which had been clouding her view of the field in front of her. Oh, the irony, now she was seeing things. Pete stood on the other side of the grassy expanse. She was going insane. Actually, maybe that was the best thing that could happen. If she saw him everywhere, at least she would remember him. However, when Mr Pearson appeared at his side, she rubbed her eyes and took a second look. Her old chauffeur had his arm in a sling but was moving with determination.

"Pete?" she questioned to no one in particular because there was no one who could hear her. "Pete." She tried to open the window to call to him, but it was locked. She ran across the room to another one, facing the same way. It too was locked. She rattled it furiously in frustration before banging to get his attention.

He finally looked her way, and the smile that spread across his face when he saw her, warmed her heart. He was here for her, and she had to get to him. She knew her father was somewhere on the property with his thugs and her soon to be husband. In an instant, she was across the room and trying the door. She'd been locked in the room when she'd first come here, but her father had been leaving it open, recently, because he knew she was too broken to even contemplate escaping. Not anymore, though. She flung the door open and sped into the corridor and down the stairs. She tried to focus her brain. From the way they were heading, he'd come in at the left side of the house. She silently cursed her melancholy nature for not allowing her to explore this place better. It was near the kitchen, though, she knew from the smells wafting her way. There'd be a door. Her heart leapt at the thought of freedom.

"Miranda." Her father's demonic voice froze her to the spot. "Where do you think you're going?"

She turned slowly to face him, the hatred she had for him bubbling beneath the surface of her body. Her mother hung off his arm like the trophy she was. On the other side was the man she was to marry. Something snapped –years of oppression and hatred surged through her with a strength she didn't think she'd ever have. This man took her baby. He had her cut open. He'd treated her like dirt all her life. No more.

"I'm leaving." Her head went high, and her shoulders squared when she spoke.

Her father raised a seemingly knowing eyebrow. "You are, are you? And where will you go?"

"With me." Pete's voice came from behind her, and his arms snaked around her waist. He rested his hand gently on her stomach as if knowing she was still tender in that area, despite healing well from the operation.

"You again. I'd hoped you'd succumb to your injuries. I see my men didn't beat you hard enough. I'll have to get them to double their assault this time."

"I don't think so." Mr Pearson appeared next to Miranda with a gun pointed directly towards her father. She looked up at him with shock, and when she looked back at her father, she noticed the expression on his face was similar. The look on her mother's face surprised her more, though, for it was a look of awe at the turn of events.

"What is going on?" the man she was to marry asked. "I said I would take her on but not if I'm to have this hassle before I even get her into bed."

Pete's hold on her strengthened, and Mr Pearson fired a warning shot into the wall behind her intended.

"Fuck this!" the man exclaimed and made for the front door.

"We have an agreement!" her father shouted after him.

"Not if I'm going to get shot at. I don't need the hassle when I can buy another woman with a lot less trouble."

Mr Pearson shot again, and the man she was to marry left at a more rapid pace.

"You'll regret that." Her father pushed her mother aside and bore down on them. Mr Pearson shot at his feet, missing by millimetres.

The two hired thugs ran into the hallway with their own weapons drawn.

"Go." Her former chauffeur turned his head towards where she and Pete stood.

"Jim?" Pete questioned.

"Go. Run. Make her free. Love her forever and give her everything she deserves."

"No." She tried to protest as Pete dropped his arm from her waist and took her hand instead. He pulled her towards the door just as gunfire filled the room, again. "No!" she screamed and looked back just in time to see her mother jump in front of a bullet, intended for her father. She fell to the floor unmoving. "Mum." She tried to pull back, but Pete held her too tightly.

"Go," Mr Pearson ordered again, and Pete tugged on her arm. She knew if she stayed, she'd die just like her mother was now probably doing.

"Miranda, please," Pete whispered into her ear. She turned to him with tears streaming down her face and nodded. In mere seconds, they were running through the corridor and into the kitchen and safety.

"Kill him." Her father's voice bellowed behind her and shivers went through her body when a hail of gunfire followed.

She had no time to process what was happening. She weaved through the kitchen with Pete, knowing her father's men would be on their trail soon. They emerged into the fresh air, and even though she wanted nothing more than to stop and vomit, she knew she had to push on. He led her into the forest with a call of 'over there' behind them. Before long, they arrived at the Cortina he'd spent his money on all that time ago.

She let out a loud cry of relief at seeing the car.

"Get in," he ordered and jumped into his own side. The instant she closed her door, he pulled away, spinning the wheels and kicking up the forest floor.

Her father's men appeared, and one of them went flying over the windshield when Pete floored the accelerator and roared out of the grounds of her father's property. She was at the point of hyperventilating, but it didn't seem they were being followed.

"It's ok. Stay calm. It's not over, yet. We need to get to Gretna Green."

"Gretna Green?" she asked.

"Yes. Once we're married we're free."

The journey should have taken half an hour, but at the speed Pete was driving, it seemed to take no time at all. She was tired, and her incision hurt from all the exertion, but she was on the verge of freedom. When the car pulled up outside a blacksmiths, she looked over to Pete.

"Are you ok?"

He placed his hand over her stomach again.

"I had a boy."

"I know. Ryan. Beautiful name."

"How?" she asked and leaned closer into him.

"Your mother. She's the one who told me where you were."

"What? Why?" The news her mother had saved her gripped her heart in spasms of pain. "I don't understand."

"We tried to save her. To make her stay behind, but she said she couldn't. I think that's why..."

"...She jumped in front of the bullet: to die. Death was preferable to life."

"She's been through so much."

"But if my father had died?"

"She wouldn't have been able to survive without the only life she knew."

"I can't believe it had got so bad. I knew he was a monster but..."

"I believe she hid a lot of what he did to her from you. Your mother was too far gone to live. I know that sounds horrible, but with her last breath, she made sure you were free. Mr Pearson also. They're the true parents you need to remember, not the man you called father." Pete pulled her into his arms and kissed the top of her head.

"We're parents."

"We are. Our little boy is out there somewhere, and I'm not going to rest until we find him. It may take a few months or a few years, but before either of us die, we'll know our son again. We'll tell him we love him and none of this was our choice."

"I'm scared."

She brought her hand to the locket around her neck.

"Marry me, Miranda."

She gripped the locket tightly in her hand.

"Yes."

PART TWO

CHAPTER ELEVEN

Miranda

"Should I ask why my daughter is sitting there silent and with a face like thunder, or is it best that I don't know?" Miranda enquired from the leather front seat of the SV Autobiography Range Rover they were travelling. She turned around to where her daughter, Sophie, glared daggers at Grayson who was both the driver of the vehicle and Sophie's husband.

"Because my husband's an arse..." Sophie started to speak but her husband interrupted

"Fifteen."

"Motherfuc...." her daughter countered, but Miranda found herself interrupting this time.

"Sophie. Not in front of Ash."

Eight-year-old Askhii, Grayson's son from a previous relationship with the now deceased Sally Bridgewater, looked up from the film he was watching on his iPad.

"It's alright, Grandma. Mum is just upset with Dad because he wouldn't let her wear a dress she liked for the flight." Miranda's heart warmed to hear the little boy call her Grandma.

"It was a one of a kind. He seems to forget that as the wife of a world-famous movie star I need to look good at all times." Sophie's pout deepened, and Miranda couldn't help but be reminded of the 'diva-strops' her little girl had been well known for as a child.

"It showed too much leg. Argue again, and it'll be twenty." Grayson did not take his eyes off the road, but the twist of his lip showed that he was enjoying the playful interaction with his wife.

"It showed the right amount of leg!" Sophie kicked the back of the chair like a petulant child.

"Twenty."

"Mum, tell him."

Miranda knew exactly what the count of twenty meant, and she really didn't need to think that her daughter would find it hard to sit down after her spanking later. She was just grateful that Ash had gone back to his iPad. The boy had developed so much since he'd moved in with Sophie and Grayson. The first few years of his life had been spent in foster care after his mother sold him to the highest bidder when born. The evil bitch was dead, now, and no one needed to ever worry about her again. If Ashkii asked about her one day, Miranda knew that Sophie and Grayson would only talk favourably about the woman, even if they both hated her. The fact that he called her Grandma, and Sophie Mum, was all she focused on because it meant so much to them all.

"I'm not going to get involved in your arguments. Your father would tan my backside for interfering in a Dom's rules."

"Mum! Yuck!" Sophie cringed, and Miranda turned back to face forward in the front passenger seat. She couldn't help but notice the wide smirk on Grayson's face at her comment, though.

"Grandma, is Grandad already at Uncle James' castle?" Ash placed the iPad down on the seat beside him and leaned forward into the space between the two front seats.

"He is. He went ahead with Uncle James to make sure everything was prepared." They were on the way to her son James' castle in the Yorkshire Dales. A few weeks ago, Pete had asked her, following a romantic dinner at an eighties revival evening, to renew their vows. The relationship between them hadn't always been easy. For a short time, they'd split up, and the relationship between them had been incredibly strained. James had been brutally assaulted by his ex-girlfriend's brothers because his sexual preferences were slightly wilder than the norm. Her son was a Dominant, hell it ran in the family. Her husband had demonstrated tendencies at the start of their relationship, but over the years it had developed, and they enjoyed a healthy sexual relationship, despite her reaching the age of fifty a few months previously. Age was nothing but a number to her, now. She felt as young as the couple sitting in the car with her. After the assault, her husband had made a mistake that threatened to tear them apart. He'd slept with a consort. It was a bitter and difficult time, but she and Pete had been through so much at the start of their relationship that no matter what, they were destined to be together forever. She forgave him, after a lot of grovelling on his part, because he was her heart, and she was his. With the addition of James and Sophie, that love had grown to become a family. They never forgot the missing piece though. She brought her hand up to the locket she still wore around her neck. She never took it off unless an emergency arose and it was necessary. Pete had been true to his word, and they'd searched high and low for their son Ryan but always came up with dead ends. She'd not seen her father since the day she fled Dumfries and married Pete. A few days after the wedding, Pete sent her father a copy of their marriage certificate along with a signed declaration that the marriage had been consummated and received word back that she was no longer to have anything to do with her father. If he saw her again, he would have her forcibly removed from his property. She knew that day she was finally free of the man who'd tormented her for most of her life. Her father died a few years back, an apparent suicide by gunshot to the head. She knew better, though, by the way Pete had returned home to her the night of her father's death. He was defeated. She'd asked no questions, not even of Matthew Carter, her son's bodyguard and best friend, who'd spent the day with her husband. James and Sophie didn't know of the existence of their brother who was out there somewhere, hopefully alive. She and Pete had made the decision to keep it from them, due to the traumatic nature of the events surrounding Ryan's birth. James and Sophie had grown up knowing Elsie and Ken, Pete's parents, as their grandparents. They'd never asked questions about her parents, accepting that they'd *died* before they were born. James may have searched further when he came into his billions. In Matthew, he certainly had the ability to do so, but he never mentioned anything, and she never asked. Ryan was her and Pete's secret, and one they rarely spoke about together because while missing him so much, it was the only way they could function, at times. He would be thirty-three now –so many missed years.

"Mum, you ok?" Sophie tapped her on the shoulder, and she came out of her memories with a start. "I'm sorry –have we upset you?"

"What? Sorry? No. Not at all. I see every day how in love you are. I'm missing your father. I've got so used to being with him all the time, again."

"We'll be at the castle soon. I'm sure he's waiting for you. I spoke to James earlier, and he said that Dad had a mopey face on him most of the time."

"I think it's probably more your brother is the mopey one from the lack of sleep associated with another newborn."

"Oh, but Isabella wouldn't annoy her daddy while she's a crying baby. She'll wait until she's eighteen and dating."

The entire car burst out laughing as they all knew that James was in for one hell of a ride when Isabella reached the age at which she discovered boys. Despite being only a month old, she was already the most stunning baby. She had the same big blue eyes as Amy, her mother. James had once told Miranda that Amy's eyes were one of the things that had first attracted him to her, now, daughter-in-law.

"At least I don't have to worry about that with my boy." Sophie placed her arm around Ash and pulled him into her. "He's going to be a mummy's boy for life."

Grayson snorted a laugh.

"Hey." Sophie lightly kicked his seat again.

"Thirty," Grayson mischievously proclaimed.

"You're kidding me. I didn't do anything."

"That's a matter of opinion."

Miranda rolled her eyes.

"How do you live with these two, Ash?"

"Headphones and an iPad, Grandma."

Grayson flipped on the indicator to come off the motorway and drive down into the Dales. The automatic car revved as it pushed up into the mountain passes but the noise coming from the engine sounded strange. Grayson looked back into the wing mirror, undoubtedly checking on the car behind them, containing his security detail. He had just returned his focus to the front of the car again when a loud crunch echoed through the vehicle. Miranda watched as he slammed his foot onto the brake pedal, but the car didn't slow.

"Shit!" he shouted out and flicked a switch on the car to turn it from automatic to manual to use the gears to slow down. It didn't work, and at considerable speed, Grayson fought to keep the car on the road. At that moment, Miranda had never been so grateful for the stunt training the young actor had received.

The car behind them sped up, presumably the driver had realised something was wrong and was attempting to overtake on the narrow roads so that he could keep oncoming cars out of the way. Grayson looked around, trying to find some other way of slowing the car. Miranda was watching him, but when she looked up, she realised they were heading straight for a sharp bend that veered off to a shallow drop below.

"Grayson," she screamed, and he looked up.

"Brace," he shouted.

Out of the corner of her eye, Miranda saw Sophie bring the still seat-belted Ash over her lap to shield him, so he couldn't see what was happening. Miranda protected her own head within her arms as the car slammed into the bend, travelling at twice the speed it should have been going. Time seemed to stand still as she peered out from between her fingers. Grayson was fighting with the wheel, and Sophie screamed as the car ricocheted off the side of the road and spun around. The tires screeched on the ground. Grayson was punching the brakes with his feet in the hopes they'd work again, but it was to no avail. She felt the car continue to move forward with the force of inertia. If it went over the side of the mountain, it would fall onto the side that Grayson and Sophie were sitting. She felt herself lurch forward, and the seatbelt tightened against her shoulder and stomach, holding her as safely in place as it could, under the circumstances. The car was sliding along the ground, now, and the air bags deployed preventing their heads from smashing against the seats.

The car continued to slide along the ground for what seemed like forever. She could hear screams coming from her mouth, but everything was surreal as if she was in a dream and all this wasn't really happening. The car hit the edge of the drop, and she felt it slide over and down. They were going to die! Thoughts of Pete, James, Amy, Thomas, Isabella, and finally Ryan flew through her mind. The car jolted and with a horrendous sickening crunching noise, ground to a halt. Her body juddered with the motion of the crash, but she was alive. Her breaths came out ragged, and she tried to clear her thoughts.

"Sophie." Grayson's deep timbre was filled with fear.

"Ok. Bleeding, but ok."

"Ash?"

"I'm alright, Dad. My arm hurts."

"Miranda?"

She looked at her son-in-law, the shock of what had just happened starting to kick in.

"Alright," she stammered.

"We need to get out. The car is full of fuel, and the lines could be cut. Miranda can you open your door?" Grayson released his seatbelt and reached back to assist Sophie and Ash to undo theirs. She didn't move.

"Miranda?" Grayson spoke again.

"Mum?" Sophie sobbed.

"She's in shock." Grayson's voice sounded muffled as Miranda tried to focus. What had he said to her before? The door..... that was it. She twisted in the seat, her side was hurting, in fact pretty much everything hurt now. She pushed at the door, but it wouldn't budge. The angle they were at meant she needed more strength to open it because it was going upward not outward. She could feel it giving, though.

"I'm not strong enough," she told Grayson as everything flooded back into clarity.

"Good to have you back, Mum," he reassured.

"Grayson?" A call from outside the car.

"Mike?"

"Yes, Boss." It was one of his bodyguards.

"We're all ok. Can't get the door open, though."

The next thing she knew, the door was being thrown open, and the familiar face of one of the bodyguard's she'd seen at the airport appeared. Sirens started to wail in the background.

"Mrs North," the bodyguard addressed her and reached over her. "Put your arms around me. I'll pull you out."

She instantly did as instructed and felt her seatbelt loosen. Grayson had undone it. The bodyguard pulled her up and out through the window as if she were light as a feather. He passed her over to another bodyguard, who was behind him, and he helped her clamber down.

"Can you walk, Mrs North?"

She nodded –her legs felt like jelly, but she knew she'd be able to stand on them.

"There's a clearing over there. Make for that."

The sound of the sirens grew louder and then stopped, presumably turned off when they arrived at the spot from where they'd just fallen. Shouts sounded from above.

"Down here," Mike called out.

"Sophie."

"Mum's coming out behind me, Grandma."

Ash slammed into her side. He had tears in his eyes, but she could tell he was trying to be really brave and not cry. She took his hand and led him towards the clearing where she'd been directed. Sophie followed. She was limping and being supported by one of the bodyguards.

Grayson was the final person to be pulled free from the car. His face was marked with cuts from the shattered glass that had smashed in from his driver's side window. His bodyguard helped him down from the car, and they all walked at a quick pace away from the vehicle as the police and ambulance crews appeared in the clearing.

Miranda looked down at Ash who was still cuddling into her leg.

"It's ok. You're safe."

Bang.

A loud explosion ripped through the air, and they all ducked. The car had exploded. Grayson and his two body-guards, who were still close to the vehicle, were propelled through the air and landed with great force on the ground. They weren't moving.

"Gray!" Sophie screamed and despite the fact she had been limping moments earlier, raced back through the clearing to her husband, closely followed by Ash. On seeing Ash run after his mother, Miranda's own legs began to carry her towards them.

"Ash, stop."

"Daddy," the little boy called out, completely ignoring her.

One of the policemen raced past her and grabbed Ash before he could go any further. The spirited child was desperate to check on his father, so he kicked and screamed, but the officer was stronger.

"Grayson." Sophie slid to the floor next to her husband, and Miranda, who was now assisting with keeping Ash away from what could be a horrendous sight, watched on with bated breath.

Eventually, after what seemed like forever, Grayson groggily started to sit up. Miranda let out the breath she didn't realise she'd been holding as Sophie wrapped her arms around her husband and smothered him in kisses. The policeman let Ash go so he could join his parents. Gradually, the other men shifted, and Mike, Grayson's bodyguard, got to his feet and came to her side.

"You alright, Mrs North?"

She looked up at him. He had a massive bruise forming on his head, and his clothes were scorched from the explosion, yet he was asking how she was.

"I'm fine," she answered before collapsing on the floor with shock.

CHAPTER TWELVE

Pete

Pete was quicker racing through the hospital than his son who trailed behind him.

"Miranda North." He pushed aside a lady who stood waiting at the reception and used his intimidating height to elicit answers about his wife.

"Sir, please. I'm dealing with this lady first." The receptionist looked at him over her thick rimmed glasses. She was one of those ladies who would normally terrify you, but he was already scared enough.

"Yeah. Wait your turn." The other lady pushed him back and glared at him, a stare that had him wanting the ground to open and swallow him.

"I'm so very sorry." James stepped up beside them and flashed the welcoming North smile. "We've just received some very distressing news about my mother and sister. My father is slightly aggravated to see them."

"No excuse for rudeness." The woman with the evil stare responded and pushed them both out of the way to resume her conversation.

"Boss," Matthew, his son's bodyguard, called, flicking his head for them to follow him. "I got hold of Grayson's man. They're this way."

Pete shoved his son in the direction that Matthew had indicated.

"Move quicker," he urged his son as they made their way through another white-walled corridor in a hospital that seemed like a never-ending maze.

"Dad, calm down. If you go in there like this, then it'll upset Mum."

"I just need to see for myself they're ok."

"I know." James stopped, bringing him to a halt also. "Dad, the bodyguard who called said they're all fine. Shaken but alright."

"I know. It's just..." He felt the emotion within him welling up. When the call had come in to say that his wife, daughter, son-in-law, and grandson had been in an accident, they'd been decorating the banquet hall for the vow renewal. He'd wanted to do as much as possible for her so that she could just enjoy the experience. Their first wedding, though beautiful, had been associated with so many mixed emotions, leaving them unable to rejoice in the occasion.

"I know, Dad. I've been there with Amy. Mum's ok."

James brought him into an embrace. He and his son may have had their issues over the past few years, but these had been resolved and the affection between them and their close relationship as father and son was now stronger than ever.

"You've got to be kidding me. Grayson! We've just been in an accident?" Sophie's indignant voice echoed through the corridor.

"I'll make it thirty-three if you carry on. Now sit down and let the doctor look at your ankle. I'm fine. They're just superficial burns."

"No." Pete winced as his daughter's elevated reply had people looking towards the room he guessed the couple were in. "Look at his burns first."

"Enough, Sophie."

Pete pushed the door open to find his daughter being forcibly examined by a doctor while her husband stood over her. His clothes were tattered and burned away in places, the skin underneath red and raw. Ash sat on a chair in the corner of the room, wrapped within the arms of Miranda. She looked up when they entered the room and let out a small sob.

Sophie stopped struggling when she saw them and allowed the doctor to look at the wounds she appeared to have on her head and ankle.

"Grandad." Ash leapt from Miranda's arms and came running to him. Pete picked him up and cuddled him closely. Ash wasn't blood, but damn, he felt like it.

"Are you looking after Grandma for me?" Pete asked him.

"The doctor said she's got something called shock. They gave her a cup of tea, and she seems a lot better now. Matthew?" Ash addressed the bodyguard, who was standing next to him and assessing the little boy for injuries.

"Yes, little man?"

"Can you get Grandma another cup of tea? I think two cups is better than one. They wouldn't let me go and get her one."

"Of course. You want anything?"

"Lollypop? Just to overcome my shock."

"Of course." Matthew winked at him and walked out the door.

Pete placed Ash back down on the ground and led him back to where Miranda was seated. He stroked his hand down her cheek and leaned in to kiss her on the lips.

"You ok?"

She nodded, and her eyes filled with unshed tears.

"Calming down. I was so scared." Her voice broke on the last words.

"You're safe now."

He kissed her again.

"I love you," she whispered to him.

"I love you, too," he responded without hesitation.

"Sophie, listen to the doctor." James' voice boomed out.

"Grayson was the one sent flying through the air by a great big fireball. They should be looking at him and not me." His daughter sobbed.

"Back in a minute," he reassured Miranda before getting up.

"Pumpkin," Pete addressed his daughter. Grayson and James, who'd been standing around her hospital bed, parted to allow him through.

"Daddy, tell them to check Grayson out first, please," Sophie cried. "He's being a stubborn Dom."

"No, he's looking after you. You've got a head wound. The doctor needs to look at that first."

"But Grayson could have one. He flew so very high." She let out a big whimper, and her husband brought her into an embrace.

"The doctors checked me thoroughly before bringing me here. They need to check your head now, and then they can patch me up."

Sophie sniffed back her tears.

"When I saw you go through the air, I thought I'd lost you."

"I know." Grayson kissed the top of Sophie's head.

"Come on, little sis." James jostled her shoulder. "You know that Gray is made of harder stuff than that. He regularly does stunts like that on film sets. Now, let the doctor take you for scans. They need to check you've got a brain in there."

"Hey." Sophie whacked her brother, and Pete knew in that instant that his daughter was calming down.

The accident had been a shock for them all, but apart from a few cuts and bruises, they all looked to be in one piece. It could've been a lot worse, but he wasn't going to think about that.

Matthew returned with the tea and a lolly for Ash. He'd also brought a coffee for Sophie. He made another trip and returned with coffee for the rest of them. Pete drank his, sat next to Miranda with his arm wrapped around her shoulder. Sophie was wheeled out of the room to undergo a head scan, and when the results came back negative for any issues, steri-strips were placed over the cut to close it. Her ankle had swollen terribly, but a scan also confirmed that it wasn't broken. It was placed in a brace, and she was told to keep off it for a few days. That led to even more tears from his fashion-conscious daughter because it meant she wouldn't be able to wear the new Jimmy Choo shoes she'd bought for the vow renewal. Grayson had his wounds cleaned. He had a rather large burn on his back, which he was told may require surgery if it didn't heal properly. He was given strong painkillers and ordered to rest. He assured the doctor both he and Sophie would do so. Ash was checked over and given a clean bill of health. He was a little upset that he didn't get to have a cool bandage like his mother and father, but when the nurse found a sticker, proclaiming him the best patient ever, he wore it with pride. Miranda was the last to be examined. She'd whacked her hand against the dashboard when the car tumbled, and it was swollen with a sprain. She was bandaged up and also told to rest.

Grayson's security team arrived with a fleet of cars to transport them back to the castle for the night. Pete travelled with Miranda in one vehicle. His wife leaned into him and allowed the exhaustion of the day to send her to sleep. Grayson had asked Sophie to travel with James because when Ash had seen they were to go in a car again, the young boy had turned as white as a sheet. Grayson travelled with him in a car driven by Matthew because, according to Ash, the bodyguard was the best driver. Sophie had slept most of the journey, it seemed, but Ash had held on firmly to his father, clutching him more tightly whenever the car made any unusual movements. Pete had seen the worry on Grayson's face when they'd arrived at the castle an hour later.

"He'll be alright. It's a lot to take in plus he's tired. We'll get some of Mrs Aimes' food into him then bed, and he'll be right as rein tomorrow. You'll see, children recover a lot quicker than we do."

"Thanks, Dad." Grayson acknowledged his advice with a weary smile.

Later in the evening when the women had retired to bed, Pete sat with his son and Grayson by the fire in the library. Grayson was nursing a brandy in his hand and staring deeply into the fire, lost in thought.

"How's Mum?" his son asked him as he brought over the bottle of brandy to refill Pete's glass.

Pete took a long gulp and allowed the amber nectar to soothe the tension threatening to erupt into a migraine.

"She's fine. Just tired. You know your mum. Tea solves everything."

"It's the first thing I told Amy about her." James chuckled and resumed his seat.

"We'll get them all involved in the vow renewal preparations tomorrow. It will distract them from the fact they'll no doubt be sore in the morning."

"Just don't mention shoes," Grayson added with a smirk.

"Sophie still distraught?" James questioned.

"I may be phoning Jimmy Choo personally tomorrow and asking him to bring out a line of ankle braces just for Sophie to wear at the wedding."

They all laughed. Sophie being concerned more about her footwear than her injury was a sign she wasn't allowing the situation to distract her from looking good.

Matthew entered the room with his brows furrowed. James got back to his feet and poured his friend a drink.

"Andrew still not going down?"

"He's cutting his first tooth. Sonia's going to sit with him for a while. I needed to talk to you." Matthew took the glass and sat down on one of the armchairs by the fire.

"What is it?" James leaned forward and placed his elbows on his knees. His features narrowed with concern.

"I spoke to the officer investigating the crash."

Pete also leaned forward at those words, and Grayson came out of his reflective state.

"It would seem the brakes were tampered with," Matthew continued.

"What?" Pete exclaimed. James hissed in a sharp intake of breath. Grayson just looked down into the now empty glass he held.

"I suspected that," the Native American said solemnly.

"I've done enough advanced driving courses for my stunt driving. I know when something isn't right. What about my inability to slow the car down with the gears?"

"Manual override was also impacted. You didn't stand a chance. If it had been a bit further up in the dales, with some of the drops there..."

"Don't," Pete interrupted, the brandy churned in his stomach, making him nauseous. "I can't think about that."

"Any ideas why? Who?" James was the practical one amongst them. He'd been through so much in his life it still left him devoid of emotion, at times, but never when his wife was concerned.

Matthew shook his head.

"Anyone had any issues they haven't told me about?"

They all shook their heads. The only problem Pete had ever had in his life was to do with Lord Braybrooke, and he was dead now.

"Do you think it's to do with Sophie?" Grayson asked.

"Sally Bridgewater?" James added.

"What?" Pete knew nothing of what they were talking about.

"No. I don't think so," Matthew replied, appearing deep in thought.

"What's going on?" Pete enquired.

Grayson nodded his head towards James to speak.

"There was an incident, recently. It was Sophie who killed Sally Bridgewater," James explained, and Pete gasped.

"What?"

"It was an accident and couldn't have happened to a more deserving woman if you asked me, but it did happen." James shrugged.

"I don't...is she ok?"

"She has nightmares, sometimes, but we're dealing with it," Grayson reassured him.

"Ok." Pete tried to quieten the dumbfounded way he was feeling about this revelation.

"What do you suggest?" James asked Matthew.

"I want to put you all on lockdown until I can investigate more. Nobody comes or goes without my say-so. It's not going to be difficult while you're here. I'm going to double security around the castle. Grayson, can I get some more of your men over here?"

"Of course." Pete was aware that Grayson had a large security retinue in America but only travelled with a few guards when he came to England because he knew James had a crew of his own to protect his family. Even Miranda and Pete had people who followed them around. James took no chances when it came to the safety of his family since the incidents involving him and Amy. Sometimes it was restricting, but Pete and Miranda went with it because they knew it allowed their son to relax and be happy with his life.

"You do whatever you need to do. I'll transfer an additional amount over to your account to cover the cost." James told Matthew.

"Are we still continuing with the renewal ceremony?" Pete asked.

"Yes," Matthew replied instantly. "That doesn't change. We need to tell the women about the extra security details because, let's face it, the second I tell Sonia what's happening, then Amy will know." Sonia was Matthew's partner, but she'd been Amy's bodyguard, at one time. Now, she was Amy's friend and confidant. The two of them discussed everything together, which Pete knew was sometimes a bone of contention with their men.

All three of the men nodded to show agreement with Matthew's response.

"If it's ok with you, James, I'd like to call in a friend of mine from MI5. He's helped us out a few times, and I know he's taking a break from government security, at the moment. He could be beneficial in finding out what's going on.

"Jasper?" James asked.

"Yes. I know this may sound strange, but too much has happened over the last few years to us all. It's beginning to not feel like coincidence anymore." Matthew got to his feet and placed his empty glass on the sideboard.

"What are you saying?" Pete asked.

"James' attackers coming back. The issues with Sally. Marie and Callum's problems with those thugs. Even my wife coming back from the dead. Something just feels wrong." Matthew stated, his face marked with tension and confusion.

"You think they're all linked?"

"As much as I hate to say it, I'm beginning to think so, yes."

The room fell silent. All four men lost in their own thoughts and worries for their families. Each had something to lose, and the fact that there was someone after them tore them all apart. Pete just had to hope they were all strong enough to face what was coming for them.

CHAPTER THIRTEEN

Miranda

Miranda shifted in the bed when she felt it dip with the weight of Pete getting in. She opened her bleary eyes and peered across the bed to where he lay. She still couldn't believe after all these years he was still beside her. In those moments of desperation when she was pregnant with Ryan, she had thought she'd never see him again.

He turned and saw she was awake.

"I'm sorry. I didn't mean to wake you," he apologised and pressed a kiss to her forehead.

"It's alright. I've only been sleeping lightly anyway. Whenever I fall asleep, I feel the motion of the car rolling again."

"It'll take a few days to recover. I remember when I had that crash in Cindy. I felt like I was spinning for days afterwards."

She smirked at the mention of his old Ford Cortina. The car had become a lifeline to them, and they were both devastated when she'd met an untimely demise, as the result of a patch of ice on a road outside Cambridge, fifteen years after they'd got her.

"Are Sophie, Ash, and Grayson alright?" she asked.

"All sleeping. Grayson put Ash's mattress in the room with him and Sophie, so they could keep an eye on him. He was a little reluctant to go to sleep as he feared he'd have nightmares. He's only eight, and it's frightened him. Give him a few days, and he'll bounce back."

"I think it scared us all." Miranda brought her hand to the locket around her neck. She could've died, today, and never had the chance to find Ryan.

"I'm still looking."

"I know." He brought her closely to him. He smelled freshly showered, something he always liked to do before bed no matter what. A hint of brandy was still on his breath, though. The men she surrounded herself with were all alpha dominants. She could picture them all downstairs, brandy in hand, discussing how they would protect their women. She allowed herself to be calmed by this vision and laughed.

"What?"

"Nothing."

He raised an eyebrow at her. Not a knowing one, but the type that said she was going to be in trouble if she didn't tell him the thoughts running through her head. Lies earned a spanking. It was an adage she knew both her children lived by, especially Sophie who, it seemed, had a constant problem with sitting down comfortably.

"Okay," she huffed. "I was thinking about you and all the boys"–because let's face it they were boys compared to Pete– "downstairs with brandy in hand and putting the world to rights."

Her husband chuckled, and she felt it vibrate through her body –such was their closeness as she lay cradled in his arms.

"It was a bit like that. James, Grayson, and Matthew are definitely alpha males, and through them, I've learned a lot about how to look after the woman I love."

"Oh yeah?" Miranda pushed up on his chest to allow herself to come to a sitting position. He moved his arms, placing them behind his head. "What have you learned exactly?"

"That's for me to know and you to experience." Miranda rolled her eyes when her husband finished his sentence with a waggle of his eyebrows.

"Well then, give me that experience."

Pete's face turned serious.

"You need sleep to rest and recover."

"I need you inside me and moving at a rapid pace. That's what I need. A damn good fucking to take away the spinning feeling. Leaving my head totally spaced out from coming instead of stressing."

"Wow!" Pete exclaimed. "It still never fails to get me from semi-hard to hard enough to bang nails in, in a few seconds, when you stop being prim and proper and demand what you need in such a dirty way." Miranda could feel her cheeks start to blush. Despite the intervening years, Pete still made her feel like the young girl he'd fallen in love with before they'd experienced the scars of losing their baby. She suppressed the thought. Her mind was awash with different emotions since the accident, and she knew she needed Pete to fuck her into oblivion, so she could sleep like a log.

"Fuck me...." She paused and thought carefully about the next word she was about to say before expelling it from her lungs with breathless lust, "Sir."

It was a clear night with the full moon shining in through the windows. She'd always liked to sleep with the curtains open since her time in the dungeon. Initially, it had been difficult to get used to the light nights during the summer, but the sun setting at ten pm and rising at four am no longer bothered her. Although the light in the room was dim, now, she saw Pete's eyes darken at her words.

Before she had a chance to register what was happening, she was flipped over onto all fours.

"If it gets too much for your wrist, just say," Pete whispered into her ear.

"What are you going to do?" she moaned back at him when she felt his hand slide between her thighs and the folds of her sex. She'd slept in one of Pete's t-shirts for so long, now, she never wore anything else. Even during the brief period they were apart, she still used an old one he'd left behind. It was so faded and tatty by the time they'd reunited that Pete incinerated it and gave her a new one with great pride. Neither of them had the perfect bodies. Her hips had birthed children and had never quite gone back to the slimline version of her youth. Pete was going gray on top and a few too many cakes were starting to leave a little extra weight behind despite the fact he worked out regularly. They were normal people their age, not the fantasy created by plastic surgery, and she wouldn't have it any other way.

Suddenly, she felt Pete's hand smack her bare bottom.

"Ouch." She shifted, but he pulled her hips back closer to him.

"That's for thinking I'm no match for those thirty-year olds down the hallway."

"I never said that," she protested, and he smacked her again. "What was that for?"

"Nothing other than the fact my handprint looks sexy on your backside." He pulled her hips into his groin, and she felt his hardness ready for her. "Do you trust me?"

"Yes." Miranda didn't need to hesitate on her answer. She trusted him implicitly.

"Red?" he questioned.

"Stop all activity, no resumption," she replied.

"Amber?"

"Stop and discuss."

"Green."

"Go for it." She allowed the edges of her lips to curl up into a playful smirk.

"Let's play, then." Pete jumped from behind her on the bed, and she shifted back around so she could watch him.

"What are you going to do?" She saw him retrieve one of her scarfs from the wardrobe and a box from a drawer.

"Matthew and I had a bit of a discussion on the way up here. He gave me some ideas. As well as a lecture on making sure I treat you right. I think he's got a soft spot for you." Pete collected a glass of water and came back to the bed.

"He misses his mother. It's been a little while since he's got over to France to visit her, and ever since she lost her arm, he's been really concerned with how she copes with the disability." When Matthew's long thought deceased wife had reappeared a while back, his parents had been caught in the cross-fire. His mother had lost her arm due to gunshot wounds, and his father had lost his ability to think properly after he was shot in the head. The two of them lived with relatives close to Bordeaux, so he knew they were well cared for. He went to visit as often as he could, but it wasn't always possible with his job and now Andrew.

"Maybe we can get James to bring his parents over to stay for a little while?"

"I'll talk to him. Anyway, stop distracting me."

She raised the fabric of her t-shirt to display herself to her husband. Her folds shimmered with her arousal.

"Fuck me!" Pete exclaimed and dropped everything he was holding onto the bed.

"I was rather hoping you would fuck me?" She laughed, and her husband pounced on her, pinning her to the bed. His hands roamed over her body while their lips joined and savoured the taste of lust that they both had for each other.

"Damn, I love you." Pete pulled away and brought the scarf into his hands. "I'm going to blindfold you."

"Green," she replied and allowed Pete to first remove her t-shirt and then put the blindfold over her eyes.

"I want you to lie back and part your legs," Pete ordered with an authoritative tone, sending shivers straight to the throbbing bundles of nerves between her thighs. "Relax."

She shut her eyes, despite having the blindfold on, and listened to his movements. She felt his breath on her body when he leaned in closer to trail a path of kisses from her breasts to her pussy. He stopped where she knew the small scar from her caesarean was and pressed extra kisses to it. The blemish wasn't big but could be seen. Thankfully neither James nor Sophie had ever asked questions about it when they were younger.

Pete lowered the path of his mouth, now alternating between kisses and small bites, setting her skin on fire. Her body tingled with the anticipation that being deprived of her sight provided.

When Pete trailed his tongue up the length of her sex, she groaned in pleasurable desire. He wrapped his mouth around her pussy, and she felt him eating her out like she was a final supper laid bare for his decadence. She could feel the orgasm building within her. It wouldn't be too long before she'd be quaking underneath his mouth from a powerful climax. He pulled away, though, and the disappointed groan, which left her lips, earned her a smack to the side of her hip.

"Pete," she squirmed, the response from her husband doing nothing to calm her need for satisfaction.

"No coming until I say, and it's not time yet."

The whimper that left her mouth was strained with frustration.

She listened closely to Pete fumbling around with something on the bed, and she remembered the small box he'd retrieved from a drawer. Wrapping was removed, and then whatever he had was swirled around in the glass of water. She could hear it hit the sides of the glass. When the cold droplets of water fell onto her pussy, instinctively, she went to shut her legs, but Pete rested between them creating a barrier that prevented her from hiding away. A pressure pushed against the entrance to her sex. It wasn't Pete because it felt different —no, it was a toy. She opened her legs wider to allow him to nudge the device inside her. It felt large, and she stretched to accommodate it. When seated, he allowed her time to adjust to the intrusion before taking her wetness and sliding it down to her puckered entrance. They'd done anal several times before, but not recently, and it surprised her.

"Relax," his gravelly voice warned, and she complied with several deep breaths. Next thing she knew, there was pressure at her other hole and a device slipping inside.

Her entire body felt like it was on the knife's edge of an orgasm when a click sounded, and the devices were switched on. The gentle movements stimulated her and left her feeling incredibly full. Pete shifted on the bed, and she felt the head of his cock nudge at her lips.

"Colour?" he questioned.

"Green," she breathlessly replied with the force of an orgasm already building rapidly down below. She opened her mouth and welcomed his cock inside her warmth.

"You're going to take all I give you. I'm going to feed you my cock until you swallow it deeply and choke." She felt him push inside her, to the back of her throat. Sucking Pete's dick was one of her favourite pastimes, and he often commented that she was worthy of the title 'better than a porn star' when it came to fellatio.

"So full," she murmured around his length, her tongue licking up and down the ridges that framed his penis. Pete grabbed her hair and took control of her movement. He fucked her mouth with wild abandonment, all the time increasing the speed on the vibrators buried in her pussy and arsehole. She was glad he'd taken charge because she damn near lost her mind when the orgasm she needed tumbled into her with a dramatic climax. She screamed around his dick as he buried himself deeper and came in her mouth. His essence coating the back of her tongue and running down her throat. She swallowed as much as she could, but his love for her was too much, and her mind was flying too high with the pleasure cascading through her body. His cum flooded out of her mouth and dropped down her chin and onto her breasts. Pete pulled back, allowing her to gasp for breath and fill her oxygen-starved lungs.

"Are you ok?"

"Yes."

He leaned forward and checked before turning the devices off and removing them from inside her. She whimpered at the tender feeling of her body. He pulled the blindfold away from her eyes and helped her to lie back.

"Time for you to sleep." He jumped off the bed and went to the bathroom to retrieve a wet towel, which he used to clean her. He dropped it onto the floor and climbed in next to her before bringing her into his arms and settling in for sleep.

"Thank you," she murmured, her body exhausted and her mind finally starting to switch off. "If you let me sleep for a few hours, then we can go for round two."

Pete chuckled and kissed the top of her forehead. "Not sure about that, my love. I think you're mistaking me for the thirty-year olds down the hallway."

She tried to raise her arm to pat his chest in a playful gesture of annoyance, but her body was already well on its way to the world of slumber.

CHAPTER FOURTEEN

Miranda

"Mum have you seen my Tiffany bracelet?" Sophie delved deeper into the bag in front of her and started to throw the contents over her shoulder. "I know I brought it with me. What the hell have I done with it?"

Miranda couldn't keep the laugh in any longer. It erupted from her at the same time as Amy's and Sonia's. This exact scenario was reminiscent of her daughter's wedding day when she panicked and lost her garter. Amy placed down the brush she'd been using to style her long blonde hair into a fishtail plait and got to her feet. She wandered over to the dresser behind Sophie and picked up a box.

"Is this it?"

Sophie nodded enthusiastically.

"Thank you. For a PA, I'm a such a forgetful clutz at times. Amy, I love you." Sophie hugged her sister-in-law.

"I hope in a different way to your brother." Amy screwed her nose up, and the laughter bellowed out again.

Thomas, who was approaching eighteen months and had been walking with that cute toddler amble for a few months, now, teetered over to her. He started a conversation that probably made so much sense to him but was still nothing but babble to her. Amy had fallen pregnant with her second child very quickly after her first but was coping well with two children under two. She'd given up the day to day management of her dancing school to her friend Elena but remained an executive partner for when she was needed. Often that need involved her leaving the children with Miranda and just catching a moment's breath by dancing for an hour. Her writing was something she continued with but without the pressure of having to identify when her next release would be. For all intents and purposes, Amy North was a full-time wife and mother and couldn't be happier. Miranda brought Thomas onto her lap, and he showed her the new car that he'd been given by James.

"Brmmm." Or what sounded like that came out of his mouth.

"Yes, cars go broom."

"Careful Miranda, he's just eaten a rusk. He could have dirty hands." Amy came to her side, grabbing a towel on the way.

"It's alright. When you're a grandma, you have to expect a few grubby hand prints, even on your wedding vow renewal day."

Sophie let out a laugh and slammed her hands over her mouth.

"What?" Miranda asked.

"Nothing."

"Sophie? Do I need to tell Grayson to add five to his current count?" Miranda raised a playful eyebrow, and Thomas, sensing the mischievous nature of the moment, clapped his hands and bounced up and down on her lap.

"You wouldn't!"

"Then spill."

"I hate being the baby in this family. You're all supposed to tease Amy, now. She's younger than me." Sophie moaned.

"I think you'll find they tried when I first married James. I'm not as easy to do it to as you."

Sophie stuck her tongue out.

"Fine, all I thought was that it isn't just when you are a grandma you get grubby hands on you on your wedding day. I'm pretty certain by the time Grayson had finished with me on our wedding day my dress was filthy."

"Oh my god, I don't need to hear that!" Miranda exclaimed.

"Well you shouldn't have asked." Sophie placed her hand on her hip and wiggled her eyebrows.

"Glad I did, though, as it reminds me of just what your father and I got up to last night and will definitely be repeating during the next few days. I'm not leaving the bedroom."

All the other women in the room placed their hands over their ears and started to sing,

"La, la, la."

"Just because I'm a few years older doesn't mean we've stopped doing it."

"Mum, please."

Sonia coughed to clear her throat, and they all looked at her.

"Is it still as intense?" she asked.

"Is what still as intense?" Miranda wanted to clarify. From what she'd heard, Sonia and Matthew were more into a masochist style of BDSM.

"All of it, the feelings, the dominant nature of the partner, the orgasms." Sonia blushed a little red on the last word.

"Yes. Does it stay that way?" Amy asked this time and lifted Thomas from her lap when he held his arms up to his mummy.

Miranda went quiet for a moment. She needed to think about her answer. So much had happened between her and Pete, but the love they shared for each other still grew if that was even possible. Once she collected her thoughts, she knew her answer.

"It gets better. More intense, more dominant, more orgasms."

"Ewwww." Sophie shuddered, and they all started to laugh again.

Miranda felt a tear come to her eye. Before she could rein it in, the pearl slid down her cheek.

"Mum." Sophie came running to kneel in front of her. "What's wrong?"

"Nothing." More tears fell —so many thoughts started to run through her head but the main one to emerge was the memory of the night long ago when Pete had returned from visiting her father with Matthew. He'd given her no details of the visit other than her father was dead, and he didn't know where Ryan was. She'd not asked at the time because she wasn't ready to face more talk of her father and what had happened to him. She was ready now, though. She needed to know and before the renewal. There was a door in her life that had to be closed before she could embrace the future. "Go get your father."

"What?" Sophie spluttered. "Mum talk to me, please. What's wrong?"

"I promise you it's nothing bad. I just need to ask him something before the ceremony."

Sophie's voice was almost a whisper, "Is it about when James made him leave?"

"No. That door is closed. I just want to ask him about something from our youth."

"About the ice-cream?"

They'd told James and Sophie the story of the first time they'd met as children when they'd been at Broadstairs with their families on holiday.

"Yes." She nodded.

"I'll go," Amy offered. "I think James can look after this little monkey, so we can get dressed properly."

Sonia got to her feet.

"I think Matthew can take Andrew for a while, as well. He seems to think he needs to run the security despite the fact Jasper and all of Grayson's men are here. He can relax and take the day off for once."

Sonia and Amy left the room with their sons while Isabella remained sleeping silently in her crib in the corner.

"Mum. You promise me you're ok."

"I'm not calling the vow renewal off. I promise."

There was a knock on the door.

"That was quick. Come in!" Miranda shouted out.

But instead of Pete entering, Jasper, Matthew's ex MI5 colleague, appeared.

"Can we help?" Sophie asked.

"I'm sorry to disturb you. I was asked to give you this." Jasper pulled a package from behind his back. "I think it's a present, which has arrived for you. Security have apparently cleared it."

"Thank you." Miranda took the box and placed it down on the dressing table. "I'm sorry if the trouble we're having is upsetting your original plans for your time off. I must say we're so grateful to have you here, though. Matthew assures us you're a fantastic officer, so we feel incredibly safe in your hands."

"You've not impacted on anything, Mrs North. I'm honoured to help. Matthew and I worked closely together in the past. He had my back every time, and I've got his, now."

"You're a wonderful man." She reached out to squeeze Jasper's hand in a show of gratitude but was a little shocked when he pulled back quickly.

"Sorry. I have issues with touch," he explained, and she nodded.

"Jasper," Sophie interjected. "You've got strong muscles. Do you think you could help me move Isabella and her crib down to the main reception room? Might as well get her settled down there for the wedding."

"Good idea." Jasper smiled at Miranda's daughter and effortlessly picked up the crib and cooed at Isabella when she momentarily stirred. They tiptoed silently out the door.

She was finally left alone to catch all her thoughts. The castle had been a hive of activity since first thing this morning, and she was still feeling a little sore after the car accident. There was a knock at the door, and Pete popped his head in.

"You alright?" His eyes were filled with worry.

She nodded and motioned to the bed.

"Aren't we supposed to do that bit after the ceremony?" He wiggled his eyebrows suggestively.

"That's not what I asked you here for."

"Damn"–he rearranged himself within his pants– "what

is it?"

She took a seat on the bed, and Pete came to sit next to her.

"I want to know what happened the day my father died."

Pete's face fell.

"Honey, why drag up the past, now? It's long since buried."

"I need the closure. I have to hear how he died before I can move on properly."

She watched him shut his eyes and let out a long breath as he made his decision on what to say.

"Everything, Pete. You have to tell me everything."

"Ok." He stood, but rather than begin his story, he went over to a dresser in their room, which she knew held hidden glasses and brandy. He poured one large glass and placed the bottle on her dressing table next to the box Jasper had brought in, reminding her she needed to open it. However, the present was quickly forgotten again when Pete walked back to her, gave her the brandy, and started his story.

"We went to see him on the premise of a business deal. You know the sort that would make him lots of money. He was more than happy to meet us. I knew the instant I walked in the room, though, he'd recognised me. Slightly ironic given he'd never remembered my face before. Obviously stealing his daughter away from him left a lasting impression, finally."

"He was just arrogant. He didn't want to know a person if they couldn't make him money. In his warped mind, you weren't on his level and therefore inconsequential and not worth remembering. The only reason he probably remembered he had a daughter was because he could sell me to the highest bidder."

"I wish I could say that wasn't true, but alas we both know differently. Anyway"–Pete shifted so he was more comfortable– "it had been twenty-five years since I'd last seen him. He'd aged so much in that time and not in a good way. For an eighty-five-year-old, I remember thinking he looked a lot older if that were even possible. He could barely walk and used a wheelchair, I suspected, as there was one in the room. His eyesight appeared to be failing, given he squinted a lot, but his mental capacity was there. He was still sharp as a tack. When he saw me, he called for security? However, Matthew was able to easily incapacitate them. I'm not proud of myself for this next bit, but the anger within me re-surfaced for what he'd done. I couldn't tamper it down. The words I used to let him know what I thought of him were ones I don't think have ever left my mouth before. They washed straight over him, though, and he laughed at me. I saw red and raised my fist ready to lash out. Thankfully, Matthew prevented me from laying a finger on him. It was what he wanted. It was at that point I calmed down and allowed my brain, not my heart, to take over. I started to tell him about our life. I showed him pictures of James and Sophie, let him know how successful I'd become in my career, and how James was well on his way to his first billion. I told him how in love we all were with life. I may have exaggerated a bit, given what James was going through with the assault at the time, but I wanted him to know everything he'd missed out on. Family, love, and devotion. But, still nothing –do you know what he asked me?"

"No."

"Did James know who he was because he needed money to repair Braybrooke Hall? I hadn't thought about it before then, but the building was in disrepair. In fact, Matthew investigated his finances after we left, and he was heavily in debt. All his scheming had failed."

Miranda ran her hand over her head in frustration.

"Money, it was always about money."

"Title and dominance but not in the way that we know it. Matthew warned him that should he ever try and contact James, it would be the last thing he did."

"I'm so glad Matthew came into our lives. I'd be lost without him."

"Yes." Pete shifted again, the tension of the conversation weighing heavily upon him. She leaned over and stroked at the back of his hand in comfort.

"It was then I asked him about Ryan. I told him if he needed money to repair Braybrooke Hall, I wanted to know where our son was. He refused the offer. Told me the whereabouts of our son would go to the grave with him. Matthew started to tear his office apart looking for information. We took copies of his hard-drive, details of his financial transactions, and when we searched back through it all, there was nothing, not one lead. It was as if our son had vanished into thin air. That was the first time I truly questioned what had happened to him. The first time I believed he might have died."

"No." She felt her heart breaking. "No, I would know. I would know if he was gone. He can't be."

"Sssh"–Pete reassured her with a kiss to the lips– "he's alive. I know it because of something your father mentioned. He told me our son had the life he deserved being the illegitimate child of a nobody. That was it....to him I was a nobody without the background or wealth that he valued so highly. It was the reason for everything he did. Pure hatred and the fear he would have nothing if he allowed us to be in a relationship."

"I don't understand?"

"We were better than him. He saw it when we were together. Your mother was the same. She was better than him, not just because of her ancestry but also in character. He was lacking and compensated in the wrong way. He was a sad man. So, I gave him a choice, thinking of him as nothing but mercenary."

"Choice?" Miranda leaned forward.

"I laid the offer back out on the table: our son for the money he wanted. I knew if he asked for a bit more than we had, then James would be able to help, so I offered him ten million. Enough to make the repairs and live out his life in peace and prosperity. He had assurances the transaction would be done without reference to where the money came from. As far as people were concerned Miranda Braybrooke had died around the same time as her mother. We reassured him she wouldn't return to society and shame him, and his good name would remain intact. I told him he could either accept the offer or choose to end his days with a pistol, but with no guarantees I wouldn't destroy his reputation. Both Matthew and I expected him to take the money."

"He chose the pistol," she blurted out, knowing that once her father had chosen a path, he'd never waver from it. That was who he was. Spite had filled him, leaving him twisted and bitter. He was a man devoid of compassion even in her childhood, but by then he would've been virtually unrecognisable.

"Yes, having kept his secret from us for all those years, to preserve his title, reputation, and property, he then chose in his final moments to increase his vindictiveness by taking it with him to the grave."

"You shot him?" She could barely get the words out.

"No. I held the gun to his temple while the room filled with his maniacal laughter. It still haunts me to this day. But, no, I couldn't do it. Matthew took over, and your father died just as he lived, full of insanity. I just hope that by taking his life Augusta and Jim can find peace in their eternal rest."

Pete looked down at the floor. His eyes filling with tears at the thought of the man he'd become such good friends with. A few years after his death, they'd discovered that her father had, at least, had him buried in consecrated ground, albeit in an unmarked grave. To cover up what had really happened the night she'd escaped from the house in Dumfries, Jim, or Mr Pearson as she still thought of him, had been blamed for the murder of her mother. It was believed that, subsequently, he'd been killed by her father's guards while they were defending their employer. Alright, it was partly the truth but there was no mention of her and Pete's role in the story. She sensed more lay behind the unshed tears in her husband's eyes.

"I'm sorry. There is something I never told you."

"What?" Her hand entwined with his.

"I had your father's coffin removed. I didn't want him to remain buried next to your mother. It would haunt her. I had it swapped with Jim's. Matthew is a master at these things. I asked, and a few weeks later he told me it was done."

She placed her hand to her face again, the knuckle of her index finger resting under her nose to help stifle the sobs.

"Thank you. Thank you. She found peace, finally. They both found it together. As for my father, it's one of the biggest insults he could ever be given. A grave of a nobody."

"You're not angry?"

"No. Not at all."

"I know Braybrooke Hall went to my Uncle, but he didn't want it and sold it to the public. It's run by a trust, which uses it as a tourist attraction. A part of me has always wanted to visit, but I didn't want to go, knowing my father was there, even though dead. Now I can. I can go and say goodbye to my mother."

"You can. I'll take you in a few days if you want?"

"I'd like that."

Pete leaned forward and pressed a kiss to her lips.

"Are you alright now?"

Miranda looked over to the antique clock on her bedside table.

"Goodness, it's almost twelve. We're to marry in an hour. Out"–she jumped up from the bed and started to shoo her husband– "Come on, out. I need to get ready."

"Jesus, woman. You're crazy." He laughed.

"Sooner we marry,"–she licked her lips- "sooner you can get me back in this bed."

"Bye." Pete turned on his heel and sped out of the door. She let out a laugh. The tension of the conversation having dissipated with the knowledge that her father had died a coward and resided now in hell. Her son was alive, and she'd talk to Matthew, again, about finding him. Perhaps, see if they could try and find some new avenues to explore. Maybe Jasper could help.

Jasper, she suddenly remembered the box. In her hurry to get to it, she tripped on a car left on the floor by Thomas. She fell forward onto her dressing table, sending the brandy and the box flying off it. They both landed with a thud on the floor, the brandy glass shattering and spilling everywhere. The lid of the box fell off, and a flash of white light blinded her. It took a few seconds to gather her senses, and when she did, the room was filling with flames. The small box must have contained something explosive, and it had mixed with the flammable brandy. The fire spread rapidly with the curtains nearby catching alight in seconds. She ran towards the doorway to her room to raise the alarm, but when she turned the door handle, she found it was locked.

"What?" she exclaimed and tried again. Nothing. She turned back to the fire, which was spreading, and thick smoke now clouded the room causing her to choke on the acrid air.

She bunched up her fist and thumped loudly on the door. She had to get out of here, or she'd be burned alive.

"Help!" she screamed. An alarm sounded outside. The fire alarms had been activated and rapid footsteps clattered along the hallway.

"Get everyone out and call 999." She heard Matthew order.

"Help!" she screamed again.

"Who was that?" a feminine voice asked in panic.

"Sonia, get everyone out," Matthew ordered.

"Ok."

"Help!"–Miranda screamed even louder– "I can't get out. The fire's in here."

"Miranda." Matthew's voice came from the other side of the door.

"Help me, please." She coughed as the thick smoke

twisted around her.

The door rattled.

"No key."

"Mum." She heard James' voice.

"Get out," Matthew ordered.

"Not fucking happening," came James' swift response.

"Stubborn arse," Matthew cursed. "We're going to have to kick the door down. Miranda, can you get to the side of the room?"

"Yes." She looked to her left and saw a space where she could take cower while they rescued her.

"Stand back,"–Matthew called seconds before what she assumed was his foot thudded against the door– "damn English oak. You couldn't have furnished the house from Ikea like any normal person."

Another thud came as she heard James say, "It's authentic."

"It's damn near impossible to kick in."

"We could use the sideboard as a battering ram."

"Not just a pretty face."

"Fuck you and help me lift this thing," James demanded.

The next thing she knew, the hammering grew louder and more regular. Her head was starting to spin from all the smoke she was inhaling, the breathable air in the room was being replaced with carbon monoxide. Finally, after what seemed like forever, the door splintered onto the floor, and Matthew's broad form filled the space. Before she could draw another breath, he had her in his arms, and they were speeding out of the castle and onto the front lawn where he laid her down on the cool grass. Sophie rushed at her with water, and Grayson who appeared to have been holding Pete back with several of his bodyguards let go of him, and her husband came to her side.

"Is she ok?"

"Is there an ambulance on the way?" She heard Matthew ask, in between her attempts at breathing fresh air into her smoke-filled lungs.

"Box," she spluttered.

"What?" Matthew bent down at her side.

"Box. Exploded. The gift."

"What's she on about?" Matthew questioned, and she grew frustrated that she couldn't manage to speak properly.

"The gift. Jasper." She tried again.

"You mean the box Jasper brought in exploded?" Sophie questioned.

She nodded.

"What's this?" Jasper bent down beside them.

"You brought a gift to Miranda."

"Yeah, a little black box addressed to her and Pete for their wedding vow renewal. Security told me it had been cleared. A man named Mike?"

"It exploded." Matthew scowled.

"What the fuck? Sorry." Jasper blushed at his language in front of them all.

"Is everyone out?" Matthew asked.

"Yes. All accounted for, including the staff."

Miranda looked at Pete –his face was white as snow. She then turned to face Matthew.

"Whatever is happening here, I think it just escalated." Matthew stood up and nodded towards James who was cradling a crying Thomas in his arms.

The sound of sirens flooded the courtyard of the castle as several fire engines and an ambulance arrived. People started to run everywhere, and she felt someone trying to examine her, but all she wanted to do was escape and hide. Why did she have the feeling that whatever was behind the attack on them, related back to her father? Even dead, he was haunting her from the grave.

CHAPTER FIFTEEN

Pete

The stale air was filled with the stench of smoke. A large section of the east wing of his son's castle lay in a mass of scorched wood and tattered timbers. Thankfully, most of the property was undamaged and still habitable. All that had been lost was a few priceless antiques. Only things, and not people. He'd nearly lost Miranda. She'd been in the room where the fire had started. His stomach turned at the thought.

The damping down took most of the day. Miranda was taken to the hospital while they assisted in salvaging what they could. The quick work of the fire brigade saved so much. He was tired and dirty, and hunger was something that had long since passed. All around him, he saw weary faces. When Miranda returned a few hours later with a clean bill of health, she was sent to rest in one of the rooms in the west wing. It was an area that was mostly used for paying guests. James rented out the castle when they weren't in residence.

He'd come back to their replacement room, earlier, to shower but had just stood staring out of the window ever since. He'd seen the fear in her eyes. It was the same look she had when her father took her away from him. Was it too much of a coincidence to believe that he could, in some way, be behind this. He was dead for fuck's sake. How could he be? Their minds were playing tricks on them – such was the exhaustion and the pressure of the last few days.

Miranda shifted on the bed. "Pete," she called out.

"I'm here." He went straight to her side and cradled her within his arms.

"Is the damage bad?"

"It's not good, but nothing James can't have his men come in and fix within a few months."

"I'm such an idiot" Miranda placed her head in her hands.

"It's not your fault." When she'd finally been able to get her breath back, his wife had told them how she'd tripped and sent the box and the brandy flying onto the floor, causing the fire. She'd been so apologetic to their son, but James had told her categorically it was in no way, shape, or form her fault. Whoever planted the explosive device was to blame. In fact, her tripping possibly saved her from more serious harm when the device could have blown up in her face. Jasper had it sent back to MI5 to see if there was anything that could be determined from it. Matthew was rather impatiently awaiting the results. The man hadn't stopped since the first sound of the fire alarm.

"But if I hadn't knocked the brandy over...."

"We'd be sitting by your hospital bed hoping you survived after an explosion in your face. Property can be replaced. People can't."

"Why is this happening? I don't understand."

"I wish I knew because I'd be putting a stop to it. None of us have done anything wrong. Not really. We're good people. It's so frustrating."

"It is." Miranda shifted on the bed. He watched her slide her legs from under the covers. She was naked, except for a t-shirt she'd borrowed from Matthew. Most of their clothes had been destroyed, and what little could be saved, smelled atrocious. They'd go shopping tomorrow, or rather they'd have a highly vetted person bring clothes to them because Matthew wouldn't allow them out of the house. Slowly, his wife padded along the wooden and rug covered floor to the new dressing table she was using. She took a long look in the mirror.

"Go get me the girls?"

"What?"

"The girls. Get them for me?"

"Why?" he questioned and joined her by the dressing table.

"Because I need them to find me something to wear, do my hair and make-up, and make me look like a bride. And if you say why again, Peter Kenneth North, then I'm going to bash you on the head to knock some sense into you."

She still wanted to get married, again. He tried to hold in the smile at her resilience. It was a beauty only he ever really saw.

"People are tired. Let's do it tomorrow."

"No." She turned to face him and placed her hands on her hips. "Whoever caused this, I'll not let them win. All we need for this wedding is the people in this Castle. They are the guests. We don't even need a priest —we're already married. All we're doing is re-affirming our vows to each other. We can look up the service on the internet, and one of the others can read it: James, Matthew, or Grayson. The girls are my bridesmaids, but if one of them wanted to do it, then they could. Pete, please. I want to do this. Now. Here. I won't let him win."

Him. The word confirmed Pete's thoughts.

"Your father?"

"Don't tell me that the thought hasn't crossed your mind. That somehow this is linked to him. The escalation just at the time of our vow renewal. We were directly targeted today. Either one of us could have opened that present."

"If it is"—Pete tried to damper down the anger rising in him— "I won't rest until I put his ghost to rest."

"That's why we have to show him we're stronger."

"I'll go get the girls."

The house was a flurry of feverish activity for the next hour. He was thrown in a shower and then squeezed into a suit borrowed from James because his was burnt in the fire. They were similar in size although his son just had a slightly narrower waistline, which needed fixing with a safety pin to extend the waist and to hold his trousers up. He was told that Miranda had a dress but from where, nobody would tell him.

Before long, they were all gathered and were ready to celebrate. Miranda took his breath away when she walked down the aisle. She was wearing the same wedding dress that, just under two years ago, Sophie had worn. He'd forgotten it had been stored here after dry cleaning. It was a princess style dress, which was full-on theatrical and gave her the appearance of being the queen and matriarch of the family that she was.

"You look amazing," he uttered breathlessly when she came to his side, and he kissed the top of her forehead.

"I can't believe I fit in it. With a couple of safety pins." She laughed.

"Believe me, you're not the only one held together with them." He winked, and she laughed back.

Their family and close friends assembled around them, forming a circle. Matthew stood off to the side, his finger to a microphone in his ear. Sonia nodded towards James who gave his best friend and bodyguard a glare, leaving the big man with no uncertainty that he was to join the circle. Matthew reluctantly handed his earpiece over to Jasper and pushed his way in between Sonia and Amy.

James started the ceremony traditionally,

"Dear Beloved, we are gathered here today..."

Pete drifted off as his son spoke. He only had eyes for Miranda, and when he looked down at her, he saw she only had the same for him. James finished his speech, and Amy took over. Miranda whipped her head around at this, and their daughter-in-law leaned in to explain,

"We're all marrying you. Your friends and family."

"Oh, how beautiful"–Miranda turned back to him– "was this your idea?"

"I wish it had been, but Sonia is the genius at work here, not me."

Miranda smiled gratefully at their friend.

Amy continued and everyone else took a turn in saying a passage from the speech they'd printed off the internet. When it came to the vows, everyone went silent to listen to them. It was his turn first.

"I, Peter Kenneth North, take you, Miranda North, to be my wife, again. I've made mistakes, so many of them, but I've never stopped loving you. My heart is yours. It's been entwined with yours since we were children. So many times, we've been forced apart, but we always find our way back together. Destiny has defined us. You've given me the gift of beautiful children"–he purposely left out the number of them, but he knew that his wife would understand he meant three and not two. They were symbiont to each other's thoughts in many ways– "a part of me and you combined."

"No sex talk," James interrupted with a heckle.

"Hush, you, or I'll make Thomas do the same to you and Amy one day."–Pete winked at his son and continued his speech– "When I first met you, you were stunning, but each day you've grown more beautiful. Until death do us part, and even then, for evermore."

Miranda wiped a tear away from her cheek.

"I, Miranda North, take you, Peter Kenneth North, to be my husband, again. I love you. I had so many words planned that I wanted to say to you at this moment, but I'm struggling not to break down. You and me. Always and forever."

He pulled his wife further into his arms and nestled her face against his chest as she sobbed.

"Oh god, we're going to need to re-do everyone's makeup." Sophie cried out her own whimper. Pete watched as each of the couples in the circle moved closer to their significant others. Hands touching, eyes looking longingly. Here, in this place and time, he was home. A heavy weight sat in his heart from the missing piece of their equation, though. His eldest son.

James stepped forward,

"We now pronounce you man and wife. You may kiss the bride."

Pete leaned over and pressed a chaste kiss to his wife's lips. He whispered, "I'll save the heavy stuff for when the children aren't around."

Out of the corner of his eye, he saw Jasper start to shuffle away. It looked as though the emotion of the ceremony had even got to the heavyset MI5 man.

"Jasper,"–he called out and was acknowledged with a dip of the head– "would you mind taking a picture of us all? I'm not sure when we'll all be together, again, with Sophie and Grayson being so far away in California most of the time. It'll be good to have one."

"Of course." Jasper pulled out his camera phone and held it up while they all assembled. Matthew and Sonia stepped aside.

"No,"–Miranda beckoned them over– "you have to join us."

"It's better just family." The bodyguard smiled back.

"If you don't think you're a part of this family after as many years of service you've put in with James, then you need your head examined, Matthew Carter."–Miranda continued– "You and Sonia are like another son and daughter to us. Please, we want you in the photo."

They both stepped forward, and everyone formed a line.

Jasper held his camera up and snapped a few pictures of them all.

"I'll send them over in a few minutes."

"Can we have cake now?" Ashkii stepped up. All the children and babies had been so quiet during the ceremony he'd almost forgotten they were there.

"Of course, we can"–Pete held his arms up– "Mrs Aimes, cake please."

The housekeeper and her family, who'd also been watching the ceremony, stepped aside to reveal a massive three-tiered cake.

"Goodness me. We'll be eating it for ages." Miranda

looked worried at the size.

"I thought it might be nice to hand it out in the village, afterwards," James informed them.

"Good idea." Miranda patted her son on the hand and stood on tip toes to kiss him on the cheek.

"Cake, cake," Ashkii and Sophie started to chant.

Grayson raised an eyebrow at them and joined in.

"Ok." Pete picked up the knife and Miranda wrapped her hand around his. Together, they pushed the knife into the cake and cut a piece, which they pulled out. When he handed the slice to Miranda, Pete noticed a piece of paper in the gap he'd left. He stuck his hand in and retrieved it. Sadly, what was written on it would turn him off ever eating the delicious dessert again.

"Mr North." Matthew stepped forward and took the paper from him.

"Fuck."

"Pete, what is it?"

Miranda was touching his cheek.

"It *was* him."

"I don't understand?"

"The message, it read, 'A touching family reunion but isn't someone missing?'."

CHAPTER SIXTEEN

Ryan

THE PAST – RYAN TWELVE YEARS OLD

"You good for nothing, lazy, disgusting brat. Why I keep you around, I don't know? It's not as though the money they give me for you is even worth it." Ryan's foster mother, Chantelle, whacked him hard around the ear, and he was sure he could feel his brain rattling around in his head. He cursed his birth parents for leaving him here. It was a daily ritual he performed in his head. His arm was still in a cast from where his foster father, Dwayne, had broken it a few weeks back. He'd been trying to help them out by cleaning the house because he knew it would make them happy. It wasn't his fault that he'd knocked into the table and sent the plates crashing to the floor, breaking them. "I'll be asking for more money to replace all of my stuff you've broken. Do you even know how much plates are?"

He thought to himself the ones he was given to eat off were probably no more than a pound from one of the cheap shops on the high street, but he knew better than to argue with Chantelle when she was in this sort of mood,

"I don't. I'm sorry." He held his good arm across himself to ward off another attack.

"You're a good for nothing freak. No wonder they gave you to me. Wish I'd said no. Get the fuck out of my sight. You can go without dinner tonight. I've got better things to do than cook for you."

He scampered out of the room as quickly as his lanky legs could take him. Dwayne was on the sofa in the lounge with the TV playing, but he wasn't watching it. The needle sticking out of Dwayne's arm told Ryan that the lights were on, but nobody was home in his foster father's head. The man was lost to his latest heroin fix. That was the true reason they kept him –it meant they could afford to stick rubbish into their veins.

He opened the front door and stepped outside onto the walkway of the run-down east London council house he lived in. There was a chill in the air. Winter was on the way, but there was no point in asking for a coat; the only think he'd be given was a beating. He wasn't enrolled in school or any clubs, and he didn't have regular meals because the people who were supposed to be looking after him weren't prepared to spend any money on him.

His stomach rumbled and reminded him he hadn't eaten since he'd had a slice of stale toast that morning. He was tall for his age, but there wasn't an ounce of fat on him. When he'd been, reluctantly, taken to hospital for his broken arm, the doctors had told Chantelle and Dwayne that he needed to have more milk, cheese, and spinach because his bone density was weak for someone his age. He had to ask his parents what spinach was because he'd never heard of it before. He was shocked there were such things as vegetables. He couldn't recall a time he'd ever had any. Most of his meals consisted of takeaways or baked beans on toast. His little belly groaned again, and he put his good hand over it to relieve the pain that spasmed through it. If Chantelle wasn't going to feed him, then he'd have to find his own dinner. He knew just the place. His long and lanky legs sped up, and he reached the back of the pizza shop, in no time at all. The delicious smells made the knot of agony in his stomach twist even more. But when he opened the lid to the first bin, a rancid smell met his nostrils.

"Nope, too old." He put the lid back on and dry heaved a few times to rid himself of the nausea induced by the rotting food.

He opened the next one.

"Bingo." The remnants of lunchtime food rested at the top of the bin. He grabbed a few pieces and was lucky enough to find some full slices that contained his favourite topping: pepperoni. It was a good day.

He brought the first slice to his lips.

"Don't eat that." A deep voice came from behind him. He spun around to see an old man watching him. His hair was white at the edges, but he was dressed well. On either side of him stood two stocky men. They were scary.

"Who are you?" Ryan asked but backed away from them at the same time.

"I'm a concerned party," the man offered and stepped closer.

"A what?"

"A friend."

"You aren't my friend. I don't know who you are. If Chantelle and Dwayne owe you money from that stuff they put in themselves, then you need to go threaten them. I don't have any money, or I'd be in the shop buying the pizza not getting it out of the dustbin." He'd learned at the age of five that there were people who would try and use him to get money from his foster parents. They'd taken him one day and kept him locked in this house with a woman who seemed to have lots of men visiting her. He'd been there for a week before Chantelle and Dwayne had shown up with a fistful of cash, and he'd been allowed to go home. He'd kind of liked it at the other house, though. They gave him food and let him watch what he wanted to on the TV. They all just laughed at him when he'd asked if he could stay there. The second time it happened hadn't been such a pleasurable experience. He'd been beaten with a stick, and it'd left a big scar on his back.

"Would you like a pizza from inside the shop?" the man asked.

"What?"

"Would you like a pizza from inside the shop? A hot one." The old man tapped one of the men beside him. "Get Ryan a pizza of his choice. We'll be in the car."

"Pepperoni!" he shouted at the man who turned to go

around to the front of the shop. It occurred to him that he should be worried the man knew his name, but he was so damn hungry he was beyond caring.

"Shall we?" The man motioned for him to follow.

"You going to hit me?" Ryan didn't move.

"Pardon."

"You going to hit me?"

"Certainly not."

"Kill me?"

"Hadn't even crossed my mind."

"Do that thing I saw Dwayne doing to Chantelle once. With his dick and pushing it in her arse."

"I can assure you that's something I'll never do." The old man's cheeks reddened with fury.

"Ok. What car you got?"

"I have a BMW."

"Cool. You've got some money."

"I have." the man agreed, and Ryan started to follow him.

"Yeah, that's a posh car. I've seen it on the programmes Dwayne watches. I like the car programmes he has on a lot better than some of the other ones. I really don't like the ones with all the women together. It looks yucky."

"Your foster father has an interesting choice of television viewing."

"Yeah. I'm not sure why I can't watch my programmes. Half the time he doesn't even know what's on."

They approached a black BMW, and Ryan let out a wolf whistle.

"This is such a cool car."

"Thank you." The old man chuckled.

The man who had gone off to get pizza reappeared. The smell distracted Ryan from the car, and he grabbed the pizza box and pulled the first slice out and shoved it in his mouth before anyone could take it away from him. It was probably the most delicious thing he'd ever tasted. He moaned with delight around the cheese and tomato goodness. Its sustenance sliding down and filling his tummy.

"Is that good?" The old man raised an eyebrow towards him.

"The best," he mumbled back with a mouth full of food.

"Good. Ryan, do you know who I might be?"

He stopped mid-bite.

"What do you mean?"

"Do you know who I am?" the man asked, again.

Ryan studied him while finishing his mouthful. He wasn't certain, but he had a few ideas. Maybe, another mouthful would help him determine the truth. He brought the pizza up to his mouth and bit down. Slowly, he chewed and swallowed.

"Are you a relative of the person who gave birth to me? The 'bitch' as Chantelle often calls her."

The old man laughed.

"I am. I'm her father."

"So that makes you my grandfather?"

The old man nodded.

"How do I know you aren't lying."

"You don't. You must trust me. I no longer speak to my daughter. She and the person who is your father are no longer allowed in my house after they abandoned you. I knew that she didn't want you, but I had no idea the lengths she'd go to get rid of you. If I'd known, I'd have never let her out of my sight as her due date approached."

"You know my father as well?"

His grandfather nodded.

"I'm sorry to say, yes. He destroyed my family and poisoned your mother against me, not that she took much persuading. It's my understanding that it was her decision to get rid of you. The heartbreak killed my wife. She died shortly after you were born."

"My grandma?"

"Yes. She would've been, I suppose."

Ryan didn't feel like anymore of the pizza. The portions that he'd eaten sat heavily in his stomach.

"Do you know where my parents are?"

"No. They left my life, and I haven't tried to contact them since. I've spent all the time I could looking for you. I came here as soon as I found you and learned about the way they've been forcing you to live."

"Are you going to take me with you?" Hope suddenly sprung in Ryan's heart for a different life. Something away from the drudgery of the one he was suffering, currently.

"Would you like to come? I'm old but can help look after you. We must be careful, though. Your parents can't find out I have you with me. They'd be so angry that I'd fear for my life and yours."

Ryan bit his lip to temper down the anger he felt at his grandfather's revelation.

"I'll be quiet. They won't know."

"Good. We can get you clean clothes and lots of food. I know you've not had much schooling. I'll hire a tutor to help you learn everything you want to know."

"Can I learn how to be a spy?" Ryan leaned forward, his eyes widening with excitement and his heart beating faster. "I saw this show the other day on the television. It was so good. The spies were so skilled, and they had cool weapons."

"If that's what you want to do, then I'll do everything in my power to help."

"Thank you." He handed the pizza box to the burly man standing next to him and flung himself at his grandfather. His thin arms wrapped around the old man's torso, and he buried his head in the man's chest. "I love you, Grandfather."

The old man stiffened, and Ryan put it down to the stress of having searched for him for so long.

"Before we go, we have to do something. Your foster parents –they can't tell anyone where you've gone."

"Ok, I'm sure I can just get in the car and go with you. They probably won't even miss me."

"No. We have to do this properly." His grandfather's

face darkened. It was a look that scared him a little, but this man was promising a better life. His current one was shitty, so at this point, he was willing to try anything. "Let's go."

Ryan jumped into the car and played with all the cool buttons that allowed him to phone someone, produce ice, and even play music loudly through the entire journey. The car pulled up outside his rundown estate, and Ryan showed them to his house. When he opened the door, both Chantelle and Dwayne were in drug induced highs on the sofa.

"Drugged up, waste of spaces." He heard his grandfather mutter under his breath.

"They're like this whenever they inject the contents of that bag into their arms. It gives me peace."

"No child should see this." His grandfather frowned and slammed his fist on the door. "Prepare two more syringes," he ordered his guards. "Be careful what you touch."

The men set to work heating up the white powder until it bubbled. They pulled the needles from Chantelle's and Dwayne's arms and re-filled them before shoving them back in.

"Done." One of the men stepped towards them. "You want us to inject."

"No."

"Ryan, do you know what'll happen to them if they take too much of this drug."

He did. He'd seen it once before when he was eight. Chantelle had taken more than she should, and she got sick. An ambulance had come for her, and he'd been hidden away. It wasn't until Chantelle had come back that Dwayne had beaten her black and blue for being so stupid and nearly dying. That is what happens when you take too much of the stuff.

"You can die."

"They haven't been very nice people to you, have they?" His grandfather pointed towards his arm. "Did he do that?"

Ryan nodded.

"She doesn't feed you. They won't let you watch what

you want. They beat you. They call you names. Do they deserve to live?"

He gasped.

"I can't."

"Why not? Have they ever shown you one kind moment? One kind word?"

He tried to think hard, but every memory he had of the two people who'd raised him since birth involved violence, drugs, and hatred.

"No."

"Do it. Get revenge for all the years of suffering. Nobody'll know. My men have made it look like an accident. Send them to hell." His grandfather's words stirred something inside him. An insane need to destroy the people who'd treated him like dirt. He needed to extinguish the memories that plagued his brain. His little feet carried him forward towards Dwayne, first, and his fingers surrounded the plunger of the needle. He inhaled a deep breath, and he pushed. Dwayne sat up. Ryan jumped back. His foster father's eyes widened, and his mouth moved but nothing came out. Then, he slid back down into the chair.

Ryan looked up to his grandfather who was smiling happily. "Well done. Now, her."

He went over to his foster mother and did the same. She didn't sit up, though. She just slumped further down into the chair. The men with his grandfather went to the two comatose bodies and checked their necks.

"Gone," one said.

"Same," the other added.

"Do you have anything that you want to bring with you?" his grandfather asked. Ryan looked around at the filthy squalor, surrounding them.

"No," he replied and followed his grandfather out to the car. They climbed in, and as the the car set off, nobody spoke. He wasn't stupid –he knew he'd just killed his foster parents. Surely, he should feel sadness or guilt, but none of those emotions were inside him. No. Happiness flooded his body, and a feeling of being free.

He picked up the box containing the remaining pizza before looking back, one final time, at what was to be his past. He pitied the poor people pulling up in the Ford Cortina, a man and a woman. They were just about to discover the sort of man he was to become.

PRESENT

From where he was stood, Ryan knew that nobody could see him. They were oblivious to him in their state of panic. The final parts of his plan where falling into place, and he couldn't be happier. His mother and father would pay for abandoning him. His siblings would bow down at his feet, and Matthew Carter would suffer for killing his grandfather before he'd had the chance to name Ryan as his heir. They would pay, every last one of them and anyone who associated with them.

They had no idea who he was or what he was capable of. He was the best of the best, a top operative in MI5, even better than Matthew himself. The idiot had just brought him right into their midst, a mistake that would cost him. He didn't use his birth name anymore. No, he lost that years ago when he took the name, Jasper Braybrooke. The heir to his grandfather's fortune until Matthew killed him before the will could be changed. He'd seen the close relationship between the bodyguard and James, and it disgusted him. Now was the time —the time to put the final parts of his plan in place. Take them out one by one, starting with James. He pulled his phone out of his pocket, pressed to dial the number he'd saved in it, and left the room. The call connected.

"Hello. I have some information for you, which I think you might find of great interest."

CHAPTER SEVENTEEN

Miranda

"Mum, you and dad need to start talking. What's going on?" James stepped up to her and folded his arms directly across his chest in a show of defiance. She knew enough about her son to recognise that he wouldn't stop until he had answers.

"James"– Amy tapped her husband on the shoulder– "let them sit down. It's a big shock. I'm sure we're all thinking things, following the message."

"But we weren't the ones targeted this morning, resulting in half my castle being destroyed."

Amy raised an eyebrow at him. "Think before you speak."

Miranda shuddered when her son growled at his wife.

"Stay out of business that doesn't concern you. Go put the children to bed."

The air sucked out of the room when Amy's expression turned to one full of thunder and fury.

"Because of the situation we're facing, I'll let that one pass, but if you ever speak to me that way again, I'll serve your balls up to you on a plate."

James shook his head and placed it in his hands.

"I'm sorry. I shouldn't have said that. I'm worried."

"We all are. Doesn't help if we start losing it amongst ourselves. I agree with you. That note meant something to your mum and dad, but they have just shared a loving event. The wind has been knocked out of them. Let them sit and work through their thoughts. They'll let us know what they're thinking when they've recovered."

James pulled his wife into his arms and kissed the top of her head. "I'm sorry." He turned to Miranda and reached out a hand to hers.

"Mum, let's sit you down. Sis, bring a drink."

Miranda went with her son to seek comfort on the sofa, but she noticed Pete remained glued to the spot. Amy went to him and nudged him tenderly towards them. Her husband wasn't fully there, though. He was reliving things in his head. When he sat, Miranda took his hand, and he looked over at her. He appeared to have aged, in a matter of moments, and his eyes were bloodshot and weary. He'd been strong for so long the pressure was finally getting to him.

"It's time." She looked directly at her husband when she spoke. "We can't protect them any longer."

"Mum?" Sophie queried, handing her a shot of whisky.

Matthew came to stand in front of her.

"We can't be certain it relates to what you are thinking."

Nothing had been directly spoken, but Miranda knew the bodyguard had read her mind regarding the reasons for what was happening.

"I know, but even if it isn't, it's time. Pete and I may not have long left. I want to go to my grave knowing that someone is still looking."

Matthew bowed his head and stepped back. James took his place and knelt down onto the floor.

"There are things that your father and I have tried to protect you from. Whether it was right or wrong to hide the truth from you, it was done out of love.

"Mum, you're scaring me." Sophie worried her lip and nervously stroked at Miranda's hand.

"Hush. It'll be ok. Just listen. I've never given you many details on my mother and father. We told you that they died before you were born, and I wasn't on good terms with them, anyway. That's only true in the case of my father. My mother, she died the day your father and I were married."

Sophie gasped.

"I was only seventeen at the time but had already been through so much. After our brief encounter as children, your father and I met again when I was sixteen. I fell pregnant shortly afterwards."

She looked at James who she could tell was doing the mental arithmetic in his head.

"Unless you've lied about your age that wouldn't be me."

"No, it wasn't. We had...have another son."

Pete jumped to his feet, and she longed to go after him, but she needed to finish her tale. He poured another glass of whisky and stood in the corner of the room. James turned to look at him and back to her.

"You gave the baby up?"

"No, not by choice. My father, he was a horrible man." She felt her throat start to tighten and a lump form at the back. "My father was Lord Charles Braybrooke. I'm of aristocratic blood. He didn't approve of the man I love, your father. He didn't approve of much that I did." She stopped to try and compose herself, memories so horrid filling her mind: the knife slicing through her stomach, the first cries of her baby, and the silence when he'd been taken from her. "He had your father beaten and hospitalised and me stolen away and hidden for the term of my pregnancy although he didn't allow me to go to nine months. When the baby was deemed viable enough to survive without intervention, he had him cut from my stomach."

This time, it was Sophie's turn to get to her feet. She had tears streaming down her face. In an instant, Grayson had her pressed to his body, providing her with the comfort she needed in that moment. Amy ensured Thomas was happy playing with Ash and came to sit on the floor with her husband. He wrapped his arm around her and pulled her in closer to him. Pete remained in the corner of the room, but she noticed that Sonia had handed Andrew to Matthew and held her hand out to Pete, allowing him to draw strength from her.

"What happened to the baby?" James' question could barely be heard even in the silence of the room.

"He was taken from me while still on the operating ta-

ble. I've not seen him since"—she broke on the last word—
"we've searched endlessly, but never found him. I know in
my heart he's alive. He has to be."

James turned to Matthew, "You've been helping them
look."

He nodded back.

"Thank you."

"What happened after that?"

"I was kept hidden away until I healed. My father came
to me and told me I would be married to a man he'd chosen
for me. Thankfully, my mother had found Pete and a friend
who'd, previously, helped us be together. Pete rescued me,
but my mother and our friend were killed. I married Pete
the same day and became worthless to my father. He never
sought us out again and died a very lonely man."

James let go of Amy, got to his feet, and walking over to
Miranda, pressed a kiss to her head. He then went to his father and pulled him into a big bear hug.

"Thank you for not giving up on her."

Sophie sat back down and placed her arm around Miranda's shoulder.

"We'll find him. Not sure how I'm going to feel about
having another brother to boss me around, but we'll find
him."

"I'm sorry we never told you."

"I won't lie that I'm not a little angry, but it's in the past.
We need to think to the future."

"We do." James led his father back over to them, and the
four of them embraced. Miranda found so much strength in
just that little display of affection.

"What I don't understand is, if your father's dead, then
why is someone coming after you?" Grayson had his hand
to his chin in thought.

"He didn't die naturally." Matthew stepped forward.

"You killed him?"

"Yes, and I think that's one of the reasons I'm being targeted as well. Sally Bridgewater knew too much about me.

Stuff that's not in the public domain."

Miranda watched Sophie wince at the mention of Miss Bridgewater.

"I think the reporter had been used as a pawn to further the needs of whoever is coming after us. Sophie, I can't prove it yet, but regardless of what happened in that room between you and her, I'm not sure she was dead when you left it."

"What?" Sophie wobbled on her feet, and Grayson reached out to support her.

"Someone's targeting us, trying to destroy anyone who's remotely related to anything we do. I think whoever did this may have started as soon as Lord Braybrooke was killed."

"But who?" Miranda tried to think of who her father would have left to do such things. The men he worked with when she was younger would be old men now and incapable of such feats.

"There's only one person I think it could possibly be." Matthew stepped forward, and Miranda held her breath. But before Matthew could answer, Pete replied for him.

"Our son."

The room suddenly exploded with men in black balaclavas and guns.

"Armed police. Nobody move." Miranda had no time to think about what her husband had just said. She held her hands in the air, immediately, as instructed. Everyone else did the same and looked around the room, stunned by what was going on.

One of the men stepped up to James and pushed him forward onto the floor. Her son knew better than to react or do anything out of the ordinary. He looked up at her from where he was lying on the floor. His eyes were wide. Another officer came over and pointed a gun at her son's head.

"James North, I am arresting you..."

"Wait," Matthew called out. "I'm ex-MI5, Matthew

Carter, there's a current MI5 operative in the building, Jasper...fuck he doesn't use a surname. Let me stand down, and you can tell me what's going on."

The man pointing the gun didn't take his eyes off James but replied to Matthew,

"You have no jurisdiction. We have information and are acting accordingly. I would suggest as you are holding your son that you hold your tongue also and let us do our job." The officer then leaned forward and pressed his gun directly against the back of James' head

Miranda saw Matthew's face drop when he realised he was helpless to prevent what was happening to her son.

"James North"–the officer started again– "I'm arresting you on suspicion of money laundering. You do not have to say anything, but it may harm your defence if you do not mention when questioned something, which you later rely on in court. Anything you do say may be given in evidence. Do you understand?"

"Yes," James replied loudly and clearly. Miranda could feel her heart beating so fast, and she was sure the air was trapped in her lungs because none was coming out of her mouth.

"Cuff him and search him."

Amy let out a loud scream when they tried to put the cuffs on. Thankfully, Isabella was in her cot, and Ash, despite his young age, had taken Thomas and was distracting him with a car. "No." She tried to race forward but was instantly restrained by a couple of other police officers.

"Amy, stay calm. We know it's a mistake. I'll explain everything and be home in a few hours. Look after Mum." James tried to keep his voice deep and commanding, but Miranda could hear the waver in it. She'd seen it in his eyes when the gun was pointed at his head.

"James," Amy sobbed, and Thomas looked up from Ash's lap.

"Dada."

Miranda knew as well as anyone in the room it was the

young boy's first proper word.

"Dada ok," James reassured him, and Amy was released and pushed in the direction of her son.

They all stood in numb silence as James was searched and, eventually, pulled from the room. Money laundering was a very serious charge. Her son was in deep trouble.

The police officer who'd arrested James went over to Matthew next.

"Better get your boss a good lawyer. This one isn't going away." The cop laughed, and they all filed out of the room. Pete and Matthew followed without a word, leaving Miranda alone with her shell-shocked family and tumultuous thoughts.

Her son. The little boy she'd cradled in her arms was doing this. It was the only explanation.

CHAPTER EIGHTEEN

Pete

"I want some information on my son, and I want it now."
Pete banged his fist against the front desk of the police reception. James had been brought straight to Scotland Yard, and they'd travelled back down through the night to be with him. Amy, Miranda, Sophie, Grayson, Sonia, and all the children had returned to his son's house in Knightsbridge to get some rest while he and Matthew had gone straight from the airport to the world-famous police headquarters.

"Sir, if you don't sit down and wait, I'll be forced to have you arrested for breach of the peace," the snotty-nosed receptionist ordered.

"You've had him for ten hours, now, and we haven't been told anything. These charges are ridiculous. My son's well known for his charitable donations to the victims of terrorists, not for providing funds to those doing the harm. I want to see a supervisor, immediately."

"Sir, everyone is busy. If you let us do our job and confirm you son's innocence, then he'll be free in no time, and you'll have the answers you seek. Now, I'll ask you one final time to sit down and wait, or I'll have you arrested."

Pete growled low in his throat. He was going to get nowhere with this job's worth.

"Be interesting to see how you can get me arrested when everyone's so busy." He turned heel and stomped back to his seat where Matthew was on the phone.

"How did they get access to his personal account? It's locked tighter than the fucking Bank of England safe?" the bodyguard shouted down the phone, and the receptionist shouted out for them to be quiet. Pete very nearly gave her the finger but thought better of it.

"This is ridiculous, Jasper. See what you can do with your boss and call me back. You know as well as I do that he hasn't done this"–Matthew continued– "ok, bye."

James' bodyguard, and best friend, hung up his phone and put it back in his pocket before turning to face Pete. "Any news?"

"The usual crap. Everyone's busy, and the receptionist's trained to not deviate from the manual they gave her when she started the job. What did Jasper say?"

"It looks like someone hacked into James' personal account and transferred money to unknown bank accounts. It only happened yesterday. I've got Jasper doing a trace to locate where the transfer was done. His boss is a little reluctant to help, though. More concerned with finding out where the money has gone and how to get it back before it goes to people it shouldn't."

"How much?"

Matthew shook his head.

"Fifty million."

"Shit."

"Yep."

The door was flung open as Callum and Marie Ashworth rushed in. Pete stood to greet them. Matthew had called James' accountant from the plane to let him know what was happening.

"Any news?" Callum asked, and Pete shook his head. "Damn. All the accounts and assets are frozen. Both the business and personal. I've had to send everyone home. We can't do anything with the business. There are police everywhere at the office, tearing everything apart."

"They won't find anything." Matthew stood up and started pacing the room. "James is as clean as they come. This is a waste of public funds." The last part was said rather loudly to make a statement.

"But it's putting doubt in people's minds. That's the whole point of this." Pete resumed his seat, and the others sat as well. "If it gets in the press. It ruins his name."

"Matthew told us what's been happening in Yorkshire, and who you suspect is behind it all." Marie spoke for the first time. Pete could tell she'd been crying. Her eyes were puffy and red.

"Yes. My first born. He's either trying to kill us or destroy us. He must think we abandoned him. If I could only find out who he is and tell him that it wasn't us."

"We'll find him. You have my word." Matthew stood. "Callum, can you stay with Pete? Just try and find out what is happening with James. He's got a lawyer in there with him, but if they're still interviewing, he won't be able to get out to talk to us."

"Where are you going?" Pete asked.

"I'm wasting time sitting around. We need to find your son, and even if it's the death of me, I'll find him by sundown."

Pete went to stop Matthew, but before he could, the big man had left the building.

"There's a Starbucks down the road. Why don't I go and get us some decent coffee? No offence, but you look like you need one." Maria stood and placed her handbag over her shoulder. "I just want to check on Owen and Olivia, as well." Pete knew that Marie and Callum were adoptive parents to Marie's four-year-old nephew Owen and parents to six-month-old Olivia. Owen's mother had been killed in a drive-by shooting when she was pregnant with him. Fortunately, the doctors were able to save the baby. Marie had lived in squalor, for a long time, when she was forced to pay back drug debts her sister had accumulated and look after her sick mother. Thankfully, she'd found Callum, and they lived happily together in Kensington, now. Both worked at James' firm: Callum as the Finance Director of North Enterprises and Marie as James' PA. Although she was currently on maternity leave, Pete knew she still spent most of her time in the office because the replacement PA providing maternity cover just wasn't up to her exacting standards, or his son's. He doubted anyone ever would be. The two of them worked so well together. James had even had the office next to his turned into a creche complete with a trained child caregiver. Often when Pete visited his son, he would find Thomas, Andrew, Owen, and Olivia in there together. He knew it wouldn't be long before Isabella joined them...but, if the worst happened, then she wouldn't. If this charge stands, then James would lose everything he'd worked for. That was a distinct possibility, anyway, if the press got wind of what was happening.

"At this point in time, I think I'm in need of a quadruple espresso. The last time I slept must have been close to thirty hours ago."

Marie touched his hand reassuringly.

"I'll get them to make it extra strong."

Marie left him alone with Callum.

"The banking world has changed so much since I took early retirement. How bad is this financially for James?" he asked Callum. The accountant's face fell.

"It's not good. The bank will have submitted a form to the national crime agency when they saw the money being moved. Even for James, fifty million is a lot to transfer, but I suspect the country it went to is the real reason for the concern."

Pete cocked his head.

"Afghanistan."

"Shit."

"Yeah."

"I've been looking through all his accounts, this morning, just checking there's nothing else that looks wrong. I think it's all ok, though. Just this one transaction."

"That's something."

"In the grand scheme of things, yes. The bank freezes the account until the crime agency has investigated. That's why I find it so strange he's been arrested. They must have had a tip off about the transaction."

"From the person who made it?"

"Would be my suggestion. I just hope they sort it quickly

because, in a few days, it's global payday. The shit really will hit the fan, then, if wages aren't sent over."

"I think the biggest problem will be keeping the media away. The stocks will have been suspended as well. I'm sure people are starting to dig."

Callum looked across at the receptionist.

"You're really getting nowhere with her?"

"Nothing."

Callum stood and motioned for Pete to follow him outside. He did so.

"What is it?" he asked when they were away from the busy reception area.

"I want to make a phone call but in there is not the right place."

"To whom?"

"The big guns."

Pete furrowed his brows together in confusion. His exhausted brain wasn't allowing him to think straight.

Callum retrieved his phone, placed it on speaker, and dialled a number. It took a while before it was connected.

"Callum?" a deep masculine voice enquired.

"Dad." Suddenly, it hit Pete who Callum had called. His father was the Prime Minister of the country.

"I've been expecting you to call," the voice on the other end of the phone informed them. "Where are you?"

"I think you already know the answer to that because I'm guessing I just interrupted a cobra meeting." Pete knew from watching news reports that this was the government's name for meetings that involved terrorist activities.

"Scotland Yard. Have they said anything?"

"We can't get past reception. Although I haven't pulled the I'm the Prime Minister's son card, yet. That's my next step if you can't give us some news."

"Us?" Callum's father halted. "Who are you with?"

"I'm with James' father. That's it. We're not by anyone else, and this call is on the private phone you gave me."

"Ok. Hello, Mr North."

"Hello, Prime Minister," Pete nervously stammered. Despite the fact the man on the other end of the phone was Callum's father, he was nervous knowing the powerful position he held.

"Dave, please."

"Dave."

"Look, you know I can't tell you everything, but what I can say is we do know this is a set up. The police need to investigate the crime and where the money has gone, but everyone here knows James in some way. He's a good man, and we don't believe the story. He is being thoroughly grilled by the police. I'm receiving regular transcripts, but between his calm nature and the solicitor he has, they've found nothing to incriminate him except for the transfer of money to a holding account in Afghanistan. That's not enough to charge him. They only have a few more hours left to interview him. I've been asked to extend his detention but declined the request. I could face issues as a result, but I'm prepared to explain my actions if I do. I know there's a man on your team with links to MI5. He needs to work together with them to find out where the money was transferred from, including finding the computer so it can be proven James has no link to it. That's the only way to prove his accounts were hacked. Once that happens, he's in the clear."

"Matthew's already working on it. He's with an agent friend of his right now."

"Good. I'll talk to the head of MI5 and ensure he has all the clearance he needs."

"No. You need to start distancing yourself from this. If people find out, questions could be asked. I'm going to get pulled into this, Dad. I'm the finance director of the company. People will go from me to you, and if they find out you've made demands like that, it could be problematic."

"You think I care about that, son? I've been Prime Minister for long enough, now. I'm done. I was going to resign on your mother's birthday this year, anyway. I've been putting everything into place. I'm tired, and we want to live the rest of our lives away from the spotlight."

Pete looked up from the phone to Callum and saw the man exhale deeply with relief. He knew that he'd grown up under the spotlight of being the Prime Minister's son, and it was a burden that weighed heavily on him.

"You don't know how happy Mum will be to hear that."

"Very. Look, my advice to you both is to go back inside Scotland Yard and wait. James will be released in a couple of hours. It won't be the end of it. He'll lose his passport and be under surveillance around the clock, but he won't have a charge against his name. Call his employees back into work tomorrow and continue as normal. The press is already asking for statements. I'm going to give them something to keep them quiet. Get James' team to do the same."

"I'll get on this straight away." Callum agreed with his father's advice.

"Just stay calm. We'll sort this out," Dave reassured. But after the last few days, Pete couldn't be certain because unless they found the person behind the plot, more troubles would surely come their way. Eventually, something would happen, and they wouldn't be able to solve it or rescue the person involved. He needed to remain positive, though.

"Thank you for your help," Pete replied.

"I have to go," the Prime Minister said, before hanging up.

"You ok?" Callum asked Pete.

"Just about." The sound of heels clicking on the pavement behind them, alerted them to someone coming. Marie appeared with caffeinated goodness in her hands.

"Why are you out here?" she asked her husband.

"Fresh air," he replied and winked at her. Whether that was a secret code between them or not, he didn't know, but Marie didn't ask any other questions. Pete followed them back inside to drink his coffee and wait. His whole body was sagging with exhaustion and worry. Marie and Callum eventually left him alone to sort out the running of North

Enterprises in the absence of his son. Pete spent the next few hours pacing the floor of the reception area. Eventually, more than twenty-four hours after being arrested, James appeared out of a side door, looking exhausted and pale. His solicitor didn't look much better. The lawyer said his good-bye, and Pete thanked him for his work.

"What happened?" he questioned his son as he led him to where a car waited for them. A bodyguard from Grayson's team had been stationed there by Matthew.

"They found no evidence to charge me. I'm not in the clear, and my assets are still frozen, for the time being. But, at least, I can go home to my wife and children. Is Amy ok?"

"Hysterical when they took you away. Sonia called a doctor to give her something to calm her down. Sophie and Sonia have been looking after Isabella and Thomas ever since."

"I need to get home to her. She's always been so scared of losing everyone after her parents' death. This would have stirred up old memories."

"In you get." Pete opened the door for James who, near enough, stumbled into the car with fatigue.

"Dad, what was his name?"

"Who?"

"My brother?"

Pete took his seat and fixed his seatbelt in place. It had been such a long time since the name of his son had left his lips, and it felt strange. He and Miranda always referred to him as their son, or firstborn, so to call him by his name seemed to hurt even more.

"Ryan. Ryan Peter North."

He inhaled deeply to centre himself from the emotion clouding his own exhausted mind.

James slumped down in the seat. "You were right."

"What?" He didn't understand.

"It's my brother doing this. The account the money went to was in the name of Ryan North."

CHAPTER NINETEEN

Miranda

Miranda didn't think she'd ever fussed over James as much as she had since he'd walked through the door this evening. He looked exhausted, and she made sure he was seated with a cup of tea in his hand before Pete pulled her away, so Amy could get near her husband.

"Sorry,"– she apologised– "over anxious mother here."

"Never apologise, Miranda. I know how hard it was for you, seeing him go through that. We know it isn't over yet, but we have him home, now. That's all that matters." Amy circled her arms around her husband. He leaned forward and placed the cup of tea on the table, having taken a sip. That pleased Miranda no end. Tea was the cure for everything.

"Do you mind if we digest everything tomorrow, please?" James stood and pulled Amy under his arm. "I'm beyond tired. I want a shower, and then I want my woman in my bed."

"James!" Miranda exclaimed, blushing.

"I don't have the energy even for that, Mum." James shook his head and led his wife down the corridor. His children were already asleep, and Miranda knew that her son would check in on them before he eventually collapsed. He was a fantastic father. Just like his father had been to him, despite the odd blip.

She turned to her husband who she was sure, by the looks of him, was asleep standing up.

"Bed." She nodded. Her own body, having barely rested in over twenty-four hours, was struggling. Pete took her hand and led her down to the quarters of the house that had once been her own private accommodation, during the time she and Pete had spent apart. However, that was a distant memory, now, and she wasn't going to dwell on it. Her husband's phone rang, and he quickly shut the door to their rooms so as not to wake anyone.

"Matthew?" Pete answered and put the phone on speaker, so she could hear as well.

"How is James?"

"Tired. Amy's taken him off to bed."

"Sonia's going to watch Isabella for them tonight. Amy's expressed some milk so that they can both get some sleep," Miranda added.

"That's my girl"–Matthew sounded tired himself– "It's only nine, so I'm going to do a few more hours work and then come back for some sleep."

"Don't exhaust yourself," Miranda told him.

"Oh, before I forget, does your family have any links to Cambridge?"

"Yes. My grandmother's family were from there, and I went to boarding school in the city. Why?"

"I was looking further into your father's accounts. I found payments to a school in Cambridge, but from the dates, they wouldn't have been related to you. I looked at security footage from around the area. It's not the best quality. Technology has advanced a lot since then, but your father is seen taking a child into the school. I can't see the kid's face properly as it's covered with a baseball cap and glasses."

"What dates?"

The other end went silent for a moment, and then she heard Matthew flipping over sheets of paper.

"1997."

"How old does the child look?"

"It's difficult to tell. Twelve, thirteen. Looks like a boy from the clothes, and he's pretty tall."

"The dates fit. It could be Ryan." Miranda had hope. Although the thought that her son was with her father started to gnaw at her gut.

"What month?" Pete asked.

Silence again.

"September."

Pete rubbed his brow as though he was willing his brain to try to think.

"That's a month after we found his supposed foster parents dead from the overdose."

"No,"–Miranda felt her legs starting to give way– "please no."

"Your father had him all along." Matthew sucked in a sharp breath.

"He must hate us. The things my father has probably told him." Tears filled her eyes.

"Matthew, please find him. We have to put him straight about everything." Pete pulled the phone closer to his ear and turned it off speaker. He walked away from her, and she stopped listening to them. Her brain couldn't take in anymore. Her father had been a demon to her when he was alive. But, even now, he was destroying her. She wasn't sure how much more she could take from him. The man had been dead for eight years and was haunting her every move, including through her son. It was the only explanation. He'd taken her little boy and twisted him into a reflection of himself: an individual full of bitter thoughts. How was she supposed to save him? Finally, she allowed the emotions of the last few days to hit her. For so long, she'd been strong, but she wasn't sure she could be any longer. The floodgates opened, and her tears fell. The sobs wracked her body, and with heaving breaths she tried to bring air into her pained lungs. Her heart hurt. Her whole body ached as she wailed for the past, present, and future in one giant outpouring of emotion. Pete ran back into the room, picked her up, and sat cradling her to his chest.

"It'll be ok. We'll find him." He tried to reassure her, but she needed this. It was her moment of weakness in so many more moments of strength. Her husband stroked her hair and rocked her closely in his arms. She felt a drop of water run into her hair, and when she looked up, Pete was crying as well.

"I failed you both."

"No, you didn't."

"I should've got to you sooner. Protected you better."

"No. Nobody knew what levels my father would go to," she pleaded with him.

"I'm not the man you needed."

"You are. You're everything I've needed. You're James and Sophie's world. They are who they are because of you. This is nobody's fault but my father's. We'll beat him, though. We will win. We'll save our son and live a life that he never had." The strength within her was flooding back with the determination to beat the man who for fifty years, now, had haunted her every move. "We'll find our son and bring him home, no matter what we discover. Our strength and love will beat the malignancy that my father has planted within his mind."

She sat up and kissed her husband. He wiped away her tears and his own.

"I need to be inside you," he whispered.

"Take me," she consented and moved so that she was straddling him. She was wearing a skirt, allowing him easy access to where she felt her body heating. He undid his trousers and pulled his already hardening cock out. No matter how often she saw it, her breath always hitched at its beauty. He pulled her panties to the side and slid her down on his length. This wasn't about taking it slow and playing with each other's bodies. This wasn't even about the art of dominance and submission. This was purely a raw need to be one on one with the man who completed her. Fate decreed they were soulmates as the only people who truly understood each other. When they were together as one, they were bonded in unity and strength. The world around them could crumble and fall, but they'd survive.

She gasped out a long breath of pleasure from the intrusion and gripped down tightly around his dick. They didn't move. Just sat staring into each other's eyes. She could feel him lengthening and hardening even further inside her.

"Always this." Pete kissed her on the nose.

"Always. Us against the world."

"Protecting what is ours."

"Ryan is ours. Us combined. We'll bring him back into our fold."

Pete slid his hands down her legs and lifted her skirt to bunch at her waist. He placed his hands under her backside and pushed her up his length.

She let her head fall back and her body become lost in the shifting of her pussy over her husband's cock. She sheathed him within her warmth as he pulled out to the tip. The movement was slow —a deliberate coupling designed to ignite their shredded nerves into fiery passion. She took over the movement herself, quickening the pace. Her head came back upright to see Pete watching her every undulation. He took his hands off her backside and pulled her top over her head. He removed her lace bra in a swift movement, freeing her breasts, which he took into his mouth. His tongue swirled over her peaking nipples, his teeth nibbling at the sensitive flesh and heightening the sensations of need coursing through her body. Her pace increased so that she was riding him like a cowgirl, taming a wild beast between her legs. Every time she slid down, her clit rubbed against him. Her breath quickened, and Pete's urgency increased. They were going to come together, their bodies entwined in need and comfort.

Pete stood and flipped them around so that her back hit the mattress. He pistoned into her harder and harder. She no longer knew where he finished and she began. He was her, and she was him.

"Come," he demanded, and her body obeyed. He was her master, lover, husband, and her forever after. She shattered in a flurry of calls of his name. Her pussy contracted around his dick as the spasms of her orgasm took over her body, obliterating the tension that had manifested itself within her. Pete thrust hard into her and stilled. His cock jerked, and he was coming, flooding her insides with his essence –warm and comforting. There was no longer any risk of further children, resulting from the coupling, so this moment had become just about them. Breathe, live, love, and hope.

Her husband collapsed down next to her and pulled her into his arms.

"I need to shower."

"I need to clean up and undress."

He kissed the top of her head, and she saw his eyes flutter shut. He opened them only for the heavy lids to close again. He was exhausted both physically and mentally. They still had most of their clothes on, but she didn't have the energy to move or to really care. Her own eyelids started to close. Tomorrow would be a new day. Matthew would find her son, they'd save him, and their family would be complete. She should make her scones. She was sure Ryan would like them. She snuggled deeper into Pete's embrace as he started to softly snore. The sound comforted her. She'd sleep for a few hours and then start baking. She might need a few ingredients, but that wouldn't be an issue.

CHAPTER TWENTY

Ryan

It was late, gone midnight, and he'd had enough of being in the company of his grandfather's murderer. Ryan wanted nothing more than to put a bullet in Matthew Carter's head like the bodyguard had done to the only person who'd ever loved him. He still remembered the day he got the news about his grandfather's death. He'd been due to go down to the Braybrooke estates to sign papers, giving him the heirship of the name and lands. Instead, he was told that he needed to leave the home he'd been living in for the last few years because it was no longer his to reside in. He'd had so much promised, and it was stolen by the man in front of him. It was a miracle he'd not killed him sooner.

"Can you check on the school manifest, again, please. It must be ready by now." Matthew swung around in the chair of the investigation room they were in and pulled up footage from the night Sally Bridgewater was killed.

"What are you doing?" Ryan nodded towards the video.

"I just have a feeling about the night the reporter died. Something doesn't add up."

"What do you mean?"

"I don't think Sophie killed Sally, but I can't explain how she died."

Matthew wasn't as stupid as he looked. Ryan had been there that night. He'd killed the intrepid reporter. She was a victim of her own selfishness, and Sophie was a casualty of her own stupidity. His sister had left the room without even checking Sally for a pulse. If she had, she would've found her alive. The reporter had regained consciousness and thought that he was there to help her. He'd been fucking the woman. She had a tight cunt despite how many times she must have opened her legs for a story. It was the only decent thing about her. She was a nasty individual as demonstrated by the fact that she gave her own son up shortly after he was born. Any woman who did that deserved to have his hands around their throat and the life squeezed out of them. He'd rejoiced as he'd watched her die. She'd made life miserable for so many people. He did the world a favour. Just like he would when his own mother dies. Some people weren't cut out for being parents. They were too selfish. Oh, Miranda and Pete made a good act of being the perfect mother and father to James and Sophie, but he knew the truth. They picked and chose the children they wanted. He didn't make the grade for whatever reason, but he was better than them and, eventually, it would show. They'd cower at his feet before he took everything from them. Death no longer affected him. How can it when at twelve years old you steal the life of the scum who was looking after you? The drugged-up wastes of space that your biological parents sold you to.

"You ok?" Matthew cocked his head at him. "You look stressed?"

"Tired," he replied and pulled up his emails to check on the manifest again. He knew his name would be on it. Not that Matthew knew his second name. He didn't use it here. To all at MI5 he was Jasper. That was it. Alright, payroll had his full details but nobody else. He didn't give a second name. He didn't have to, and nobody asked. Matthew shoved his surname in everyone's faces. 'Carter' was like a badge of honour to him, but he'd die a traitor's death. Ryan had details of every kill the bodyguard had made outside of the law, every crime he'd committed in the name of the North family, and when the man lay rotting, he'd piss on his good name by releasing it. Sonia made her bed by choosing to lie in it with Matthew. She'd have nothing when all this was over. No, he wouldn't do that to her. He had a soft spot for her because she'd suffered from parents who'd abandoned her, too. He'd see her right, but not to the same luxury she was used to. He could always do with a house-maid when he took over North Enterprises and its assets.

"It's more than that." Matthew interrupted his thoughts, again, and he tried hard not to imagine the man with his brains splattered all over the desk. If he let his mind wander, it would happen. He was that close to pulling the trigger.

"Some of what's happening is bringing up memories of my own past. I probably just need a few hours' sleep. You're right. We'll get this manifest and then rest for a bit. We'll start making mistakes if we work too hard. The first thing you learn at spy school." He laughed.

"Training seems like such a long time ago." Matthew set up a scroll on the video, and Ryan watched.

"It was. A lifetime ago."

"Why did you join?" Matthew asked, not taking his eyes of the screen. This was the way they'd worked when they'd been friends, before his grandfather died. He'd respected Matthew and vice versa. They were similar in experience and age. But the second he recognised the ammo that shot his grandfather, the respect died.

"It's a long story."

"I think we've got time. The school must have the biggest archives going, judging by how long it's taking them." Matthew laughed.

"Did you have a happy childhood?" Ryan asked and pulled up his own video to make himself look busy. He knew he wouldn't find anything on it, though. He wasn't anywhere near the property during this incident, but Matthew had insisted that it could be linked. Clutching at straws much?

"It was good. I've a large family in France, and we spent summers there. Happy memories. What about you?"

"No. I was glad to reach adulthood. The people who called themselves my parents should never have been allowed children. I was their only child, and they treated me like a slave. Beatings, and no food, that sort of thing. I was blessed the day I got out of there. They are the reason I became a spy. It allowed me to get rid of people who shouldn't be allowed to breathe the same air as us. The people out there who are sick, twisted, and far beyond being recognisable as human."

"There's a few of them out there. My dead wife for starters." Matthew huffed but still didn't move from the screen of the computer. Ryan's emotional state was becoming volatile, again. Talking about his past always made him feel that way. It was like there was a part inside him that was defective and replaced his reason when it was triggered. He'd always wondered if that was why his parents hadn't wanted him. They knew there was something wrong with him when he was born. James and Sophie seemed so sensible. Yes, James had killed but not as much as he had. His brother could step back from the voices in his head and not allow them to rule him. Ryan, however, hadn't found the way to shut them off, yet. All he heard was – 'Kill, kill, kill. Get revenge for those who have shunned you. You may not be worthy of their love, but it's them who will suffer.'. He rubbed at his temple as the permanent stress headache he'd had the last few weeks, came back with a vengeance.

"What happened to you parents?" Matthew finally took his eyes off the screen and swung round to face him.

"They're dead." His reply was cold.

Matthew lowered his head. Ryan didn't need to confirm how, when, or who had taken their lives. Matthew knew.

"Vengeance. Don't let it rule you. It's over. Put the memories behind you and move on."

Matthew swung his chair back to face the screen just as a figure dressed in black walked across it. It was quick, and in the shadows, but Ryan knew instantly that it'd be him. The computer in front of Ryan brought up a new email as Matthew frantically rewound his screen and used the swipe keyboard to zoom in.

Ryan opened the email. There it was, the entries to the school on that day. At the top of the list as if in neon lights was his name.

Matthew gasped and swung around, his chair flying backwards. James North's bodyguard knew because on the screen was Ryan's face.

"You."

He allowed his lip to curl up into a snide grin.

"Finally,"—Ryan teased— "thought you were a great detective and everything. You never had a clue."

"You killed Sally Bridgewater," Matthew spat out in disgust.

"Don't say it like you think it was the wrong thing to do. You were on the verge of doing it yourself."

"But to blame Sophie?"

"I didn't blame her. You didn't check the body properly. You've grown sloppy." He pulled his gun from his pocket and held it directly in line with Matthew Carter's chest. The bodyguard was no longer a serving member of MI5 so was frisked when he entered the building. He had no weapons, no phone, and no means of protection on him. He was a lamb to the slaughter. "Shame you had to do it after you killed my grandfather."

"Jasper"—Matthew held his hands up— "you have to listen to me. All is not what it seems. You need to talk to Miranda and Pete."

"What, for more lies? I think I've had enough of them in my life, don't you?"

"She didn't want to give you away. It was her father." Matthew was backing across the room. There was a panic button located on the wall, and he was heading for it.

"Don't lie"—Ryan snarled— "he was the only one to save me."

"No. He was playing you."

"You're sick." He tried to tamper down the voices in his head, telling him to fire. To shoot, and to end the menace to society in front of him.

"You were a good agent. One of the best. Why? Why get involved in something like this? Taking justice into your own hands. I lost everything!"

"Jasper. Please. You need to put the gun down. I can prove everything I'm saying. You must listen to me. Put the gun down, and we can go and talk to Miranda and Pete. There's no major harm done, yet. You're right, Sally deserved to die. She was a disgusting piece of work. What's happened with James can be corrected in an instant. Please put the gun down."

"Did he beg for his life?"

"What?" Matthew inched closer to the panic button.

"My grandfather?"

"No, he told us that he'd take your location to the grave so that Miranda and Pete would never know where their little boy, they'd spent years searching for, had gone. He was a bitter old man who'd been responsible for alienating himself from any family he'd ever had. You need to listen to me. Don't do this, Jasper. It won't end well. Please. Miranda needs her son."

"She has her son, the precious James North, the boy she chose. The only one who was good enough for her. Well, I guess she picked the right one, given he made billions and has kept her in a life of luxury. I would've just put her down in a blood bath." He spat at Matthew and cocked the trigger on the gun.

"No, she's a good person. You wouldn't have killed her."

He laughed so loudly that the sound echoed around the small room like an eerie cackle of a madman. Maybe that was where he was descending, into insanity. It certainly felt like it, now. Why could nobody see his grandfather for the man he was. The kind old gentleman who'd saved him from eating out of a dustbin.

"Jasper, Lord Braybrooke was a bad man. You must listen to me. What he did to Miranda, he had you...."

Bang.

The gun went off without him even realising he'd fired it. He looked from the pistol to where Matthew was standing. Red started to seep through the front of the white shirt the bodyguard was wearing. The world slowed down —he'd done it. He'd shot the man who'd killed his grandfather. His plan was coming together. Matthew made a last-ditch attempt for the panic button but failed when he fell to the floor. He didn't move. It took Jasper's breath away. He'd killed him. He'd done it, so why wasn't he elated. It felt wrong inside his chest.

No, he couldn't think that way. He had to continue with his plan for revenge. The time was nearing when he'd end it all.

Calmly, he picked up his phone and tucked the gun into the back of his jeans. His jacket was slung over the chair in the room. He picked it up and pulled it on. The leather material felt luxurious and warm in contrast to the cold feeling, spreading throughout his body. He looked down at Matthew who still hadn't moved.

"One down. Mother and father, I'm coming for you."

CHAPTER TWENTY-ONE

Pete

Pete rolled over in the bed to find it empty. He bet his wife was up at first light and baking. It was the way she coped during times of stress. He pulled the covers back and swung his legs out of the bed – he was still in last night's clothes. Damn he must have been exhausted. He pulled them off and threw them at the linen bin. He headed into the bathroom, did his business, and brushed his teeth. He'd shower later. If Miranda was baking, then he wanted what she was offering, first. Rummaging through his wardrobe, he found a pair of jogging bottoms and a Bon Jovi t-shirt from the eighties. Perfect. He dressed quickly and made his way into the kitchen.

There were no smells of baking, though.

Only Amy and Sonia talking. The latter sounded worried.

"He didn't come home, and I've been calling him, but he's not answering." Sonia nibbled on the tip of her finger in anguish.

"Who?" He stepped forward and poured himself a cup of coffee.

"Matthew." Amy opened the fridge and passed him the milk. He thanked her with a nod of appreciation.

"I'm sure he's just working hard on trying to find Ryan." James strode into the kitchen. He was dressed in only a pair of jogging bottoms. Amy licked her lips at the sight.

"Yeah. I'm sure he is, but it's unlike him not to check in every few hours or so."

"He may have thought you were still asleep." Pete looked over at the clock on the oven. It read 8:30am. Damn, he'd slept late.

"I think I'll try him again. It can't hurt." She picked up

her phone from the counter and dialled.

Sophie and Grayson entered the room, next.

"Morning," they both greeted.

Sophie took a seat at the table while Grayson poured two coffees and handed one to his wife.

They looked at the empty table, and it was then he realised that Miranda wasn't in the kitchen.

"Where's your mum?" he asked.

They all looked around.

"Isn't she still in bed?"

He shook his head. "She mentioned something last night about baking." Grayson pulled the phone out of his jeans pocket and dialled a number. Sonia was still trying Matthew.

"Mike. Mrs North...any idea where she is?"

"Yeah. She wanted to go to the supermarket. I sent her with Mark and Kenny."

"Thanks." Grayson hung up and put the phone away. He sat down and motioned for Sophie to sit on his lap. She obeyed, instantly.

"Your mother and baking." He shook his head.

"You love it, Dad." James came up and lightly tapped Pete's stomach. It wasn't as flat as it had once been. One too many cakes and hot dinners.

"I'm sure if Amy keeps cooking, you'll have exactly the same in a few years."

"Doubt it. Amy keeps me well exercised in other ways." James sidled up to his wife and wrapped his arms around her.

Sonia put the phone down.

"Still no answer?" Pete asked.

"No. He gave me a number for MI5, once. I'm going to try that and see if someone can check on him for me."

"Wasn't he with Jasper? Have you tried him?" he questioned. Sonia slapped her forehead, indicating she was stupid.

"Of course. I think I'm exhausted."

She picked her phone up and dialled a different number. "Jasper?"

Sonia's brows knitted together. Pete wasn't sure why, but a cold shiver spread down his spine.

"Jasper?"

Sonia stumbled backwards and went as white as a sheet. James leaped, from where he was holding Amy, to grab her just before she fell to the floor. He took the phone out of her hand and while supporting her put it on speaker.

Demonic laughter came from the other end of the phone. They all looked at one another, but when a feminine scream sounded, the bottom of Pete's world fell out. He knew that voice anywhere.

"Miranda." He jumped forward and grabbed the phone from his son. "Miranda."

"Hi, Dad."

Jasper's voice came over the phone.

"Jasper?" he questioned.

"I think it's Ryan, isn't that what you named me? I forget. It's been such a long time since I went by that name. Ever since my grandfather rescued me. Such a shame he was murdered. I've taken care of the perpetrator of that crime, though."

Sonia's legs completely gave way this time, and James struggled to hold her up as she registered what Jasper meant. James himself looked sick to the stomach.

"What do you want?" Pete tried to keep his voice calm.

"It's time to end this. I want you, Sophie, and James to come to the roof of North Enterprises. Just you three. Nobody else or my mother gets a bullet in her. I think it's about time we had a little family discussion. Deviate at all, Dad, and I mean it, I'll make the bitch a pin cushion of bullet holes."

"You have my word."

The phone line went dead.

Sonia's cries broke the silence in the room.

"I have to go and find him."

Grayson pulled his phone out of his pocket again.

"Mike?"

"Boss."

"I think you'll find that Mark and Kenny are dead or severely incapacitated. I need two men to accompany Miss Anderson to MI5 headquarters. We believe Matthew Carter could be"–Sonia whimpered– "injured."

"I'll have them bring a car round immediately."

"I'll need another one as well."

"Boss, what's going on?" Mike's voice was hesitant.

"We know who's doing this."

"Who?"

"Questions later. When we get to our destination, you're to stand down. Nobody is to enter North Enterprises unless they have my permission."

"Understood, Boss." The line went dead.

Pete tried to catch his breath –Jasper was his son. Why hadn't he seen it. The man had similar physique and build to James. He thought back to all the photos his mother had of relatives on the sideboard of his childhood home. He could see it now. Why couldn't he then? Jasper had a look of his uncle about him. James was different, more squared featured like Miranda's father. It was something that haunted his wife.

"I have to go. Amy, will you watch Andrew?" Sonia was already on her feet and running out of the door.

His daughter-in-law nodded.

"Wait." But it was too late. Sonia had left.

"James, you can't go there. Not alone, please," Amy pleaded.

"Sophie's not going," Grayson added.

"What? I am. That's my mum."

"And I'm your husband, and I'm not allowing you up there without me."

"Enough!" Pete shouted. He was struggling to take in all that was happening. His first born was holding his wife hostage, and Matthew Carter was probably dead. "Enough.

Please. Let me think."

"Dad?" James came up to him and placed his hand on his shoulder. "She's been through worse and survived."

"Not with her own son. She held him, James. He fed from her before he was torn away. She's lived with that memory for thirty-three years."

"And she'll have more. Good ones."

James turned to Grayson.

"Amy, call Marie and Callum, get them here to look after all the children. We're all going to the building. Grayson, I know you're trying to protect Sophie, and I'd say the same if it were Amy."

"But..." Grayson interrupted as Amy left the room to make her call.

James continued, "I'll protect her with my dying breath, if I have to."

"No!" Sophie sobbed.

"And I'll protect you both. Family, we're all coming out of this alive"–Pete stepped forward– "All of my children and my wife.

Grayson's phone dinged.

"Car's here."

Miranda

"It's beautiful up here. The view's amazing. I can see why he chose this building for his office." Ryan, the man in front of her, would never be Jasper again. Not now she knew who he was. How had she not known all along? There was so much of Pete in him when she looked at him properly. His eyes were the same shape. But thirty-three years had passed. She'd spent a life time away from him. Her baby. She couldn't help but remember his little face as it looked up at her from the operating table. She saw vulnerability both then and now when he turned to face her.

"They're here. They seem to have disobeyed me and brought Amy and Grayson. No wait. Wow, those two have just got back in the car."

"Ryan, please."

"I'm not Ryan... I'm Jasper. The name your father gave me."

"Please. Don't do this."

"Why, Mum? The guilt for leaving me starting to break into that frozen heart of yours."

"I never left you," she partly shouted despite trying to remain calm. She'd realised the moment her son had taken her and shot both her bodyguards that he was not mentally stable. His mind was twisted so badly he couldn't see truth from lie. That was how her father worked.

"Liar."

"You've listened to my father's side of the story. Will you not listen to mine?" she pleaded. He hadn't tied her up, but she was sat on the roof top. The air was cold, and the sky had darkened. It would rain soon.

"Because I'm sick of hearing your lies."

"You've never heard one lie from my mouth."

"What? You expect me to believe after all these years that you are the perfect mother? My god, you've raised a girl who can't even tie her own shoelaces without a man do- ing it for her. Sophie's a child. And don't get me started on James. He's a murderer. I know all about him and Colette Fisher's brothers. I saw what was left of Jacob's genitals. What kind of sick man does that to another human being. That's what you raised. A sick freak."

"No. Sophie's not a child. She's loved by Grayson. You've heard what she's said about their relationship. It's been well published. It may be different from the norm, but it's what they both want. She knows Grayson has her best interests at heart and trusts him to do what is right for her. That's the love they share. Conventional isn't always right.

Sometimes, it doesn't suit people." Ryan started to pace up and down the side of the roof. She knew his gun was tucked into the back of his trousers. "James isn't a freak either. He's loving and protective. Colette's brothers were freaks. They were forcing woman into lives that were against their wishes. They beat him because he touched Colette in a way that's natural. Sex isn't something to be ashamed of. It's something that happens because we love each other."

"Is that what happened with you and Dad?" He stopped pacing.

"The sex?"

"I'm not going to discuss my sex life with my son." She looked down at the ground.

"What, you embarrassed? Too late for that, Mum. You opened your legs wide, so my dad could stick his dick in your filthy cunt. You didn't like what resulted, so you gave it to people who spent the money you paid them on heroin. Do you know by the time I was five years old I could have injected myself? I'd seen them do it so often. You had your five minutes of fun. I got the lifetime of crap as a result.

"I never wanted to give you away."

"But you did."

"I didn't." Ryan jumped down from his vantage point on the roof and bore down on her. He pulled the gun from his trousers and held it out in front of him.

"You wanted me to rot in hell because I was an inconvenience."

"I wanted to love you."

"You hated me."

"I loved you."

"Lying bitch." He pushed the gun against her temple as the door to the roof opened and the rest of her family stepped out.

"Finally." Ryan pressed the gun harder. "Mum and I were just discussing how wonderful our dysfunctional family is."

"Take the gun away from her head, and we can discuss it

further." Pete walked to the forefront with James behind him and Sophie tucked away from the bullets, should they start flying. Damn alpha men.

"You don't get to tell me what to do, Dad. You're a few years too late for that."

"Maybe some discipline from a parent is what you need," Pete snarled, and Miranda felt the gun dig deeper into her temple.

"You're too much like him." Pete came over, so he was standing directly in front of them.

"Who?" Ryan asked.

"You're grandfather. Stubborn, bitter, and refusing to listen. I was there when he died. Couldn't have happened to a better man, if you ask me. He was disgusting."

"Shut up." Ryan inhaled deeply, his nostrils flaring.

"You've listened to his made-up stories. Now, you're going to listen to our truths.

"Pete, no," she whimpered. She knew exactly what her husband was doing. He was antagonising their son so that he would remove the weapon from her and aim it towards him.

"Your mother lived a life of hell under that man. He spoke down to her at every opportunity. She was nothing but a money-making venture to him. His own wife chose to die because of the damage he'd done to her."

"Pete," she pleaded, the tears streaming down her cheeks. Out of the corner of her eye, she saw that Sophie had been placed behind a pillar by James, and her son crept around the edge of the building towards Ryan's other side. What were they planning?

"She wasn't even allowed to listen to music because it spoiled his serenity and peace. Yes, we were young and made a mistake. Your mother was sixteen when she fell pregnant with you. I was going to stand by her and marry her, though. I loved her. We wanted you the second we knew you existed."

"Lies!" Ryan shouted, and a flock of pigeons scattered

from a nearby roof.

"Never. We went to your grandfather and told him Miranda was pregnant. He had his thugs beat me up so badly I spent months in a coma. He took Miranda from me that day. The next time I saw her, you'd been born. That was how long he kept us apart."

"He wouldn't. He saved me from those people you left me with."

"We never left you with anyone. He's the one who did that. We searched everywhere. Every day, we followed leads. One time, we thought we were close to finding you when we went to your foster parents' house and found them dead."

"Cortina." Ryan pulled the gun back a little.

"What?" Pete froze, his hands slightly extended into the air.

"I remember. As we were leaving, a Cortina and two people got out."

Miranda's stomach lurched, and she couldn't help but retch on the small croissant she'd eaten for breakfast that morning. Ryan pulled the gun back when she vomited.

"That was us."–she heaved– "We missed you by moments. We were too late."

"I don't understand."

Pete took a step closer to him.

"Charles Braybrooke took you back to his house that day, didn't he? Braybrooke Hall?"

Ryan shook his head.

"He said I wasn't allowed at Braybrooke Hall in case you had people watching the house and took me away, again." For a thirty-three-year-old man, his voice sounded so small and young. Her son had been taken by her father from one minefield to another. "He took me to a place in Dumfries. Later, he sent me to school in Cambridge. He changed my name to Jasper Braybrooke, so you wouldn't find me."

"Dumfries is where you were born." Miranda wiped her mouth with the back of her hand. Ryan no longer had the gun pointed at her head, but it was still close enough to shoot her if anyone made a move that spooked him.

"The house?"

She nodded.

"I thought I didn't like that place. He said that you'd discovered I was gone from the foster parents, and I needed to hide down in the dungeon room. I spent five days down there before I was transferred to Cambridge."

Why couldn't he see it? That his grandfather hadn't been looking after him. He'd been hiding him so they, she and Pete, couldn't find him. Was he so starved of love for the first few years of his life that he'd clung to the first person who'd paid him attention? Her father had known what he was doing all along. He was paving the way for this to happen. The ultimate revenge on his part. The son kills the family.

"I spent nine months in the dungeon." She'd been gentle with him up until now. But to be kind, she needed to be cruel. She had to break the fantasy he had of his grandfather being a knight in shining armour. She needed to show him the truth.

"Nine months?"

"Well, not exactly. I was probably six weeks when I found out I was pregnant, and you were born three weeks early because that's when they told him you were viable and able to breathe on your own."

Sophie poked her head out from behind the pillar. She looked devastated. James was still working himself into a position, presumably, so he could try to wrestle the gun away. She and Pete were still in prime position, though, directly in front and to the side of their son. She wanted to reach out and bring him to her chest.

"Viable. Breathe on my own."

She slowly got to her feet. It startled Ryan a bit, and he pointed the gun back towards her. She lifted her t-shirt and lowered her jeans a little to reveal the scar on her abdomen.

"They cut you out of me."

"Cut? You had a caesarean."

"Not by choice. The pain medication was not even fully working when they made the first incision."

"Lies. That could be from James and Sophie."

"You're not a fool, Ryan. You would've researched us. You know I had them naturally."

"My father pulled me out of the dungeon one day and had me strapped to a bed. He ordered a small medical team to cut you out of me."

"No."

"Yes."

Her hand went to her necklace, and his eyes followed. They zoomed in on the locket.

"You were delivered onto my chest. I held you. Your little face was all crinkly but still the most beautiful thing I'd ever seen. You were hungry, so I latched you onto my breast, and you suckled while people worked around us. I didn't even hear them or see them. People were stitching up my abdomen, and I didn't feel a thing because I had you in my arms. My son, my little boy. But, then, they took you from me. My father came into the room and had you ripped from my arms."

She looked up from where her hand was at her chest and into her son's eyes. They were filled with tears.

"No," he stammered.

"Yes."

"I got this necklace that day, and I've not taken it off since. Do you want to know what's inside it?"

"No, you have to be lying. He wouldn't; he was going to name me his heir. I was going to be his future. He saved me from the people you left me with."

"He would never have made you heir. He was setting you up for a fall." Her breathing was so fast, now, the sound pounded in her head, but she needed to keep her focus on the man falling apart in front of her.

"Stop lying," Ryan cried. Before she'd spoken, his voice was filled with anger and fury, but now it was laced with only despondency and failure. She opened the locket in her hand and showed it to him. Behind the glass plate was a lock of his hair.

"Your first curl."

"No."

His entire body deflated, and in an instant, both James and Pete pounced. The gun was wrestled from Ryan's hand and thrown across the floor of the roof towards Sophie. She grabbed it.

Ryan lashed out and punched Pete directly in the face. He stumbled backwards and into a wall, his head banging loudly against it before he slumped to the floor.

"Pete." Miranda ran towards him.

James and Ryan stilled.

"Dad." Sophie was at her father's side.

"Dad,"–Ryan stammered– "I've been so wrong."–Her son looked behind him to the edge of the roof– "I'm sorry."

He took off towards the edge.

"No!" Miranda shouted just as he went over. James was there, though, his arm extending out and grabbing his brother.

"Fuck! I can't hold on," her youngest son shouted in agony and a loud popping sound filled the air. Miranda realised that the arm James had used was the one with the damaged shoulder, caused when he was shot by Amy's evil uncle.

Sophie scrambled across the floor, and grabbing hold of her younger brother's feet, she pulled with all her might. A shadow fell over them. Grayson, Amy, Sonia, and Matthew appeared. The latter looking pale and still covered in blood. They were all there in an instant and pulling both the men from the edge. Pete stirred from his momentary loss of consciousness and was helping before she had time to register what was happening. James came back first and then Ryan.

Amy smothered her husband in kisses, despite the fact he was still cursing and screaming. His arm was out of the socket, and he couldn't move it. Sophie went to Grayson, and he brought her into his arms, holding her so tightly it looked like he'd break her. Matthew collapsed onto the ground, breathless, and Sonia checked under his suit jacket to see what injuries he'd sustained.

Pete sat next to Ryan. Both were dazed and confused. Miranda scrambled to her feet and wrapped her arms around them. In time, it changed to both her and Pete holding Ryan tightly.

"Mum, Dad." His words were those of someone seeing clearly for the first time. A broken man but with hope of repair.

"Ssh." she cooed. "It's ok. Everything's going to be ok. We've got you. Your family has you. You're home."

Amy

Amy opened the lid of her laptop and entered the password to switch it on. She'd promised James she wouldn't write while she was here, but there was something on her mind that really needed putting down on paper. She opened the word document and started to type,

---

Dear Reader,

Here we are. We've come full circle; our story is at an end. So much has happened: heartache, love, betrayal, and life. A tale that started when a girl of twenty-one boarded a plane to Lanzarote has given way to a series full of emotion. I know that you want conclusions. Loose ends tied up with neat bows so that your hearts and minds can rejoice. Well here they are:

Michael and Colette

You pretty much already know their happy ending. Our friends, yes, a word which at one time seemed alien whenever Colette was mentioned, live happily in Florida with their two children. We see them often, though. Colette is like a different person from the one I was first introduced to. She has banished the scars of her past and thrives under the love of her husband. She's finally free, and it's a glorious thing to see.

Alexia and Marco

Mistress Alexia still appears on occasion, but the Dominant within her is very much submissive to Marco. They run Grayson's Vegas club as their own, now. The branding is

the same, but the club is theirs. A gift from the actor. They overcame the expectations placed upon them by their fathers and live happily with their third child on the way.

Callum and Marie

I hated Marie when I first met her, but I guess that was the protective instincts within me for 'my man'. Now, she's one of my closest friends, and we talk each day. James promoted her after the incident with Ryan. She knew North Enterprises just as well as he did, so he made her chief executive when his previous one took early retirement. From her humble beginnings in the tenements of London's slums to one of the most powerful businesswomen in the country. Although she still bows down like any good submissive to her husband, Callum. He continues as Finance Director of North Enterprises, and his skill and knowledge combined with those of his wife have seen the company flourish. More and more, they take on the day to day running while my husband steps back to be with his family. That doesn't mean Marie and Callum's own family suffers –far from it. Olivia is now five and ruling the roost. She reminds me a lot of Sophie, and I'm sure my own son, Thomas, has a soft spot for her. Owen is nine and becoming just like his father –the adoptive one, not the biological one, I must add. I wouldn't want to confuse anyone. I think of Callum as his only father, biological or not. Owen has already stated he's going to be Prime Minster like his grandad Dave once was. David Ashworth's name is now legendary as one of the best politicians our country has ever had. He's been asked to come out of retirement several times, but he's happy just being a husband and getting under his wife's feet.

We see so much of Callum and Marie. They're trusted by my husband as members of our small inner circle. We both learned the art of submission together, taught by our skilled husbands. Our scenes together have become widely discussed within Grayson's London club. When together, Marie and I both like to be punished for topping from the bottom.

Sophie and Grayson

My sister-in-law and crush-worthy husband relocated from America back to London after everything that had happened. Grayson placed his career on hold for a while, but they didn't suffer financially, for he'd made enough from the Renegade films to last a lifetime. Certainly, enough to keep Sophie in designer dresses. She still acts the diva she is, but we all know it's her soft heart that shines through. It took her a long time to come to terms with the fact she hadn't killed Sally Bridgewater. She had blamed herself for so long and resigned herself to eternal suffering, believing her actions had taken a life. It was difficult for her to accept the alternative reality. Eventually, she worked through her issues, and the birth of her and Grayson's daughter three years ago helped. Rayen, Native American for Blossom, gave strength to both Grayson and Sophie and a little sister to a teenage Ash. The boy has flourished under the love of a family. His start in life could have damaged him in ways we've all seen the effects of, but he's probably the strongest out of that branch of my family. He's getting so big. He has the makings of his father's physique, and the girls will very soon be paying far too much attention to him.

Both Sophie and Grayson have continued to embrace their heritage, and they work hard to build better lives for people on both sides of their nationalities. Now, the couple are focused on philanthropic work, and both are actively involved in helping children from the slums and the more impoverished native reserves. Grayson still does the occasional acting job, though. He could never leave it behind, and we were all shocked, recently, when he made a guest appearance in a well-known British soap opera. He looked so funny with a pint in hand and arm resting on a bust of Queen Victoria.

In the end, though, with Grayson and Sophie, it comes down to the relationship they have between the two of them. Sophie needs guidance and submission twenty-four hours a day. She needs a master who'll be there for her, and never once has Grayson let her down. They'll be the same even in old age. He'll be putting her over his knee and smacking her backside for cheekiness, I'm sure.

Matthew and Sonia

I'd never been so glad to see Matthew as I was up on the roof top. To look at your husband dangling precariously over the side of a building, screaming out in agony because his arm is ripping from the socket.... it's the stuff of nightmares. Sonia told me she'd found Matthew lying in a pool of blood and thought him dead. She'd barely been able to breathe let alone check on him because she didn't want confirmation of the news that would destroy her. She'd lost so much in her life already, to lose the man she loved would've finished her off. She found strength, though. She felt it came to her from the heavens —from her mother and father, reunited, and forgiveness passed between them. A gunshot wound was not enough to keep a man like Matthew Carter down. He'd been knocked unconscious when he'd fallen, but somehow the bullet had avoided all his major organs. He allowed the injury to be temporarily stitched and swung into action to save his best friend, my husband. I owe Matthew more than I can ever repay. He and Sonia still live with us. It might seem strange, but we are a foursome without the sex. We scene together of course, but both men are too possessive to ever let the other one touch. Sonia and I touching, however... they seem to enjoy that. Matthew no longer bodyguards for James. He runs the security at North Enterprises and Sonia assists.

After everything that happened, Matthew went down on one knee and proposed to Sonia. She accepted, and just a few weeks later in a low-key ceremony, they became man and wife. I don't think I've ever cried so much. They celebrated in private together, and nine months later, Ben was born. Two years later, they had Chloe. Heaven help her when she's dating. Her father already gives Owen and Thomas the death stare when they so much as look at her.

My husband once said he and Matthew didn't have a normal boss/employee relationship. He was right –they are male soulmates and their bromance, if you know what I mean, was never like that. You don't get one without the other, and I wouldn't have it any other way.

Miranda and Pete

I am blessed with my parents-in-law. I don't think you could have two better people supporting you. They're the head of our little gang of friends and relatives. We feed off them for our strength.

They'd buried so much and suffered for so long. To have a child physically cut from your womb must leave unfathomable scars, but they survived and nurtured not only the man I love but also everyone else who encounters them.

Miranda still feeds copious amounts of tea to anyone who comes to her with a problem. Somehow it works, though, because when you leave her, you feel like you could take on the world.

Pete made mistakes in the past, and he suffered for them, but when he was beaten and left for dead by Miranda's father, he could have walked away. But, he didn't. He spurred a generation on by fighting for the woman he loved. Over the years, I've developed just as close a relationship with him as Miranda. I lost my true parents at far too young an age, but in Miranda and Pete, I've found new ones, and I love them with all my heart – just don't tell James I've given them the keys to the playroom on a few occasions. According to him, his parents don't have sex. I know differently. They're like rabbits and always at it.

Ryan

I should hate him. He's the reason for most of the suffering in the stories you've read. But I can't. He broke after the incident on the roof, and it took him a long time to re-

*cover. But he finally had a family, and we brought him
through the darkest days, together with Elena, my friend,
who is now the head of my dance school. But that's a story
yet to be written.*

James and I

*And so, to the final couple, we started all this so long
ago in Lanzarote. A chance encounter that spawned a series. My god, it seems like a lifetime has passed. James
saved his brother on the rooftop that day, but he made a
sacrifice to do so. One which has never left him the same.
When he rescued me from my uncle, he was shot in the
shoulder. The wound healed, but the strain of holding onto
Ryan tore the muscle apart again and ripped his arm from
the socket. They put everything back together, but he lost
the use of his arm. It's only recently he's begun to get some
feeling and movement back into it. I'll never forget the day
in the hospital when he looked at the doctor, who'd just giv-
en him the diagnosis of his injury, and asked if he'd ever be
able to hold his children with it again. I cried, and then I
cried some more, and then I found the strength to help him
get through what was happening to him. It wasn't easy at
first. My husband, as you've seen, is a proud man and likes
his independence, but he battled with so much at first. Just
dressing was a chore and seemed to be an endless struggle.
I'd stand and watch him trying until finally the defeat
would show on his face, and he'd allow me to help. One day,
though, Isabella fell over, and he was there for her. He used
his good arm to bring the other around her and wrap her in
a cocoon of comfort. It gave him the hope he needed, and
we've been trying different therapies ever since. I know despite having limited movement, now, he'll fully recover,
eventually.*

*James and Ryan, along with Sophie, have developed a
close relationship. The sibling love I saw between Sophie
and James has been transferred to include Ryan as well.
They had issues they needed to work through. Ryan suffered*

a lot of guilt over James' injury, and Sophie's distress while coming to terms with the death of Sally, but his youngest sibling forgave him easily. I love to watch them together. It brings me great joy, especially when Sophie's being teased by both her brothers.

James took a step back from North Enterprises. As I've said previously, he allowed Callum and Marie to take on a lot of the responsibility. He'd worked hard all his life to build up his business and when he was cleared of all suspicion against him and his fifty million was returned, he made the decision to semi-retire and spend more time with us. I gave my dance school over to Elena as a present. She refused it at first, but you can't hand back what's already signed over to you. I'd proven my point that I could be independent. I wasn't the little girl who had relied on her parents, and then on her uncle for everything. I'd become strong. I'd become a North. Together, we've raised our family and enjoyed our ability to just live life to the full. Thomas and Isabella were joined by two more siblings, Henry and Charlotte. After that, Matthew dragged James to see his doctor, demanding they gave him a vasectomy because contraception had this strange habit of not working with us. For a bodyguard, we were becoming too big a family to protect.

Well, dear reader, that's it. That's what has happened to all of us. We have all lived happily ever after. Giving you the ending you need, and the conclusion you love.

Thank you.

Amy started to type, 'The End', but James appeared at the door.

"I thought you weren't going to write while we were away?"

She bit her lip and looked down.

"It was only a few words."

"Come here," he beckoned, and his eyes darkened with lust. She shut the lid of the laptop and got to her feet.

With her hips swaying, she went to him and knelt down to present herself to him in slave position. "You know what happens to naughty girls?"

"They get punished."

"They do." He wrapped his good hand around her hair and pulled her to her feet. The next thing she knew, she was against the wall behind her.

"Take off your clothes."

She obeyed without question, and her white summer dress and matching panties fell to the floor. The heat of the Lanzarote sun warmed her body, or was it the stare coming from James? This was the first time they'd returned to the island since they'd met.

"Full circle," she said to him. He nodded.

"Place your hands above your head and don't move them." Once, the authoritative tone had scared her, but now it sent shivers down her body and prepared her for what would happen next.

He pressed a hot kiss against her lips, and then trailed his mouth further over her neck, and down to her breast.

"Good girl's get rewarded."

"And bad girls."

"Get nothing," he teased and lowered his hands to her thighs. He parted them and slid his finger through her wet folds.

"How long have you been like this?" he asked.

"Since you walked into my life."

He circled her clit with his thumb, and her body sagged against the wall with a jelly-like feeling in her legs.

"You don't come until I say."

"Yes, Master."

James pulled his hand away and went to the zipper of his shorts, which he undid, deftly, having become an expert at using only one hand. Sliding his shorts and pants down his toned thighs, he revealed his hard cock. Memories of the first time she'd seen it flooded back. It had been beautiful then, and it was even more so, now, because she knew how it could make her feel. He stepped out of the garments and returned to her. He lifted her left leg, and wrapping it around his waist, he positioned himself at her entrance.

"Mine," he growled.

"Forever," she replied, and he slammed deeply into her in one hard thrust.

"May I touch you?" she asked

"Always."

Amy slid her hands down her husband's back and over the skin marked with scars. Last time they had been in this position, she wouldn't have been able to do this, for he didn't allow her to touch him. He'd held her hands above her head as he'd taken her −ashamed of the scars, marring his back. That was the past, though. If he was a deviant, then she was one with him. James pulled back and found a steady rhythm as he took her against the wall. The coupling possessive and a sign of his dominance over her. She found his lips and kissed them hard. His swivelling hips brought them both quickly to orgasm. She flew high and free, her body quaking and milking his. Eventually, they both came down, withdrawing from her, James lowered her leg gently.

"Did I hurt you?" he asked, a hint of worry in his voice.

"Never."

He leaned his forehead against hers.

"We're going to be ok, aren't we?" he questioned, and she cocked her head in confusion. "For the rest of our lives, we're going to live happily."

"Nobody knows the future," she replied and led him out of the study they'd been in and towards the bedroom.

"No, I supposed they don't. We have to make it work ourselves."

"No, we have to control it."

He laughed.

"Well, Mrs North, let's control the future...together."

THE END

Thank you for reading
THE CONTROL SERIES

Coming Soon: A Control Series Standalone Spinoff
SECOND CHANCES
Ryan and Elena's Story

The Control Series: A dramatic, witty, and sensual suspense romance set predominantly in London.

Surrendered Control, The Control Series, Book 1:
Amazon US: http://amzn.to/2oMKuKo
Bookbub: http://bit.ly/SC-BB

Divided Control, The Control Series, Book 2:
Amazon US: http://amzn.to/2oNtDal
Bookbub: http://bit.ly/DC-BB

Misguided Control, The Control Series, Book 3:
Amazon US: http://amzn.to/2H0zZuj
Bookbub: http://bit.ly/MCon-BB

Controlling Darkness, The Control Series, Book 4:
Amazon US: http://amzn.to/2oExCGW
Bookbub: http://bit.ly/CDark-BB

Controlling Heritage, The Control Series, Book 5:
Amazon US: http://amzn.to/2EVtqvQ
http://amzn.to/2oGEymV
Bookbub: http://bit.ly/ConH-BB

Controlling Disgrace, The Control Series, Book 6:
Amazon US: http://amzn.to/2FhDJKO
Bookbub: http://bit.ly/CDis-BB

Controlling the Past, The Control Series, Book 7:
Amazon US: https://amzn.to/2N9UcAp
Bookbub: http://bit.ly/GRCPast

The Touch of Snow, The Glacial Blood Series, Book 1
Amazon US: http://amzn.to/2oExTJY
Bookbub: http://bit.ly/TOS-BB
Goodreads: http://bit.ly/2gQQQre

Fighting the Lies, The Glacial Blood Series, Book 2:
Amazon US: http://amzn.to/2F9HIK8
Bookbub: http://bit.ly/FTL-BB
Goodreads: http://bit.ly/2xaIa56

Fallen for Shame, The Glacial Blood Series, Book 3:
Amazon US: http://amzn.to/2FPPGoU
Bookbub: http://bit.ly/FFS-BB
Goodreads: http://bit.ly/2odGjYr

Shattered Fears, The Glacial Blood Series, Book 4:
Amazon US: http://a.co/bAe8h18
Bookbub: http://bit.ly/ShatteredFears
Goodreads: https://bit.ly/2qEh1Ei

Coming Soon to the Glacial Blood Series...
Hidden Pain – Hunter, Lily and Kingsley's story
Stolen Choices – Katia's story
Power of a Myth – Molly and Hayden's story
A Deadly Affair – Jessica's story
Banishing Regrets – Kas' story.

A dark and suspenseful series set amongst the elite of a London society intent on finding power in the wrong place.

Legacy of Succession, Dark Sovereignty series, Book 1
Amazon US: http://amzn.to/2FRo3fi
Bookbub: https://bit.ly/2vqksD5
Goodreads: http://bit.ly/GRLoS

Tainted Reasoning, Dark Sovereignty series, Book 2
Coming January 2019
Goodreads: http://bit.ly/GR-TR

A Father's Insistence, Dark Sovereignty series, Book 3
Coming April 2019
Goodreads: http://bit.ly/GR-AFI

VICTORIA

I swear I must have read the same page in this high society gossip magazine at least five times. You know the sort: who's marrying who, which couples are divorcing, and who's running around Chelsea in nothing but their bra and knickers. It's boring! But then again, it's more interesting than the life I have. The highlight of my day would be if the cook changed the strictly ordered meal plan that I've eaten every week, without fail, since I turned sixteen. Five years of the same food is enough to send anyone crazy. But I shouldn't complain. My father, Arthur Cortland Hamilton, Viscount Mayfield, is a wealthy man, and I lead a life of privilege. I've never wanted for anything: clothes, makeup, books, they've all been produced within hours of asking. My days are often spent lounging around by the indoor pool after swimming a hundred lengths, as I am now, but I want something more. I didn't go to regular school like normal people — I was educated at home by a governess. My brother, Theodore, Theo for short, went to a local private school. He would always come home with tales of the friends he'd made and the games that he'd played. My games would consist of reciting my times tables, so I didn't fall asleep from the monotony of the day. I once asked my mother why I wasn't allowed to go to school, and all she would say was 'to protect your reputation'. I have no doubt my gravestone will read, 'Here lies, the honorable Victoria Hamilton. She died from boredom, but at least, her reputation was intact.'

I give up on the magazine and place it down on the ornately carved sixteenth-century table. I take off the towel, which I'd wrapped around me after my swim. I'm dressed in only a small black bikini. It's the one I always try to choose because of the inlaid embroidery of a rose on it. It's my favorite flower.

"Miss Hamilton?" I turn my head toward the middle-aged butler when he addresses me. He bows.

"Yes."

"Miss Bennett is on the telephone for you." He hands me the phone, and I wave him away before squealing into the receiver.

"Tammy, how are you?"

She's excited about something. I can tell from the hyperventilating breaths coming from the other end of the phone.

"I did it. I've taken my last exam, and it feels so good. I'm sure I passed it. I answered nearly every question."

"I'm so happy for you. That's amazing news."

Tamara Bennett is my only friend. She's the same age as me. We grew up together. She made life tolerable in this mansion of no fun. Her mother, Elsie, is lady's maid to my mother and me. She doesn't know who her father is. Her mother tells her it isn't important. We used to make up stories that he was a hero off fighting for his country, and one day, he would come back for her and Elsie. He never did though, and the truth, about him being a father who abandoned a pregnant woman, seems a lot less exciting. Still, I'm glad she came to live with me because it means I can live vicariously through her. She's been at Oxford University for the last three years, studying law. I've missed her so much.

"All I need to do is pack up all my stuff and I'll be coming back to London."

"When?" I try to temper down my excitement a little bit, but her giggle tells me she knows I'm practically climbing the walls without her here.

"I've got a few end-of-term parties first, so a couple of weeks."

"A couple of weeks," I say sadly.

"I know. It'll go quickly. You'll see."

"I wonder if Daddy would let me come up to see you at the parties? Theo could accompany me. That way, I wouldn't get into any of the trouble he thinks would befall me if I happened to leave the house."

"Victoria." Her answer is ominous. Not because she doesn't want me to come, but she knows my father would say 'no' immediately.

"I just wish for once he would trust me."

"He does trust you."

"He doesn't," I interrupt. "He thinks that if I see a man, who isn't a relative, all my morals will go down the drain, and I'll hump him like a wild dog."

"He's doesn't think that!"

"Then, why didn't he allow me to go to University to study the History of Art? I obtained a place at Oxford. You don't get higher than that. I also had a place at Goldsmiths, which is just down the road, so I'd still be able to live at home. Every time I asked, the answer was 'no'. If he'd trusted me, he'd have let me go."

"He just doesn't want to see any harm come to you. Some parties can get a little bit rowdy." Tammy's voice went quiet on the other end of the phone.

"You've been to them?" I ask.

"A few times."

"What happens, tell me?" My living by proxy is all done through my friend, and I'm not going to let her keep details from me.

"Ria." My nickname since we were toddlers. She struggled to say Victoria when she was younger, so it was just shortened to Ria, and it stuck.

"Please," I beg.

"Ok, there was this one party when I was in my second year. It was after the end of the final year exams. Some of my mates brought in some kegs of beer. They were paid for by one of the final years, he was a billionaire's son. He had more money than sense. We spent most of the day drinking and ordering in pizza when we got hungry. By the evening, we were all pretty merry."

"Drunk?" I interrupt, not knowing what that feels like. I'm allowed a glass of wine with my dinner and champagne at the functions Daddy throws. I've never been drunk.

"I was on my way to drunk. I wasn't drunk. My inhibitions were lowered. There was this guy. We'd been working together on our final project for the term."

"Did you have sex with him?" I know Tammy isn't a virgin. She lost her cherry, when she was at school, to a guy she'd been dating for a year. She came home and told me all the details.

"Eventually. But first, we played Twister with another couple. Every time someone fell over, they had to remove an item of clothing. You know how clumsy I am. I was naked with my backside in the air in no time. One of the moves put him behind me. He got hard, so we stopped playing and fucked right there on the lounge floor. Most of the party were watching us, but we weren't the only ones naked. Lots of couples were having sex around us."

"Wow." It's all I can say. I mean I've read books about sex and looked at videos on the internet, when I've wanted to get myself off, but to be involved in a real-life orgy sounds amazing. Jesus, Tammy had such a good life. "What happened next?"

"Yeah. Next wasn't good." She goes quiet. "I found him having sex with some other girl later that evening."

"The bastard."

"It was an evening of free love. I went and found another partner."

"I wish I could do it for once."

"No, you don't. Your saving yourself for your husband."

"What husband!" I exclaim indignantly. "Don't I have to be allowed to leave the house to find one?"

"Have you spoken to your father again about getting a job?"

"What's the point?"

"You told me about the volunteering position at the art gallery. Maybe since you won't be getting paid, he'll let you?" she asks, hopefully.

"Oh that, I left the information on his desk. I went in the next day and found it in the bin. He wouldn't even entertain it, money or not." I stand up and walk around the pool to the French doors that open over our manicured gardens. We're on the outskirts of London so have a large plot compared to some, and I welcome it because it means I can escape and walk. I open them and take a breath of air.

"I'm sure he'll allow something soon. Maybe when I move back, we can persuade him to allow you to come out with me more."

"It won't happen, there's no point in asking. I'm stuck in this place. Probably until he chooses a husband for me, and then, I'll be stuck doing what another man wants me to do." I'm so down with my life at the moment, I just want to have a purpose.

"We'll think of something," Tammy offers. She knows how sad I get. "What about asking him if you can help him with his business affairs again? He was more than happy for you to help him arrange the functions when your mother was ill. Maybe you could take some of the running of the estates away from her. Talk to her."

"That's a good idea. She's been busy with Theodore and his new business venture recently, and she still looks weak after the flu." Her mother had caught flu the previous winter and had been bedridden for weeks. She had problems with her lungs anyway, from an iron deficiency at birth. It hit her hard. She spent time in the hospital and took months to recover. "I'll ask him when I next see him. Mother can concentrate on Theo, and I'll run the estates. At least I'll get to talk to people. "

"Great idea." I can hear voices, in the background, on the other end of the phone. They're calling my friend. "I'm going to have to go, Ria."

"Going on another drinking fest?" I laugh, but she goes silent. "Have fun and be careful."

"I'll be home soon, and we'll work on you being allowed out more. I promise. Go talk to your father about the estate."

She hangs up, and I go back to staring out of the window. Our gardens are formal in style. A rose border dominates the vista from the pool. It's June, and the beautiful pink and red petals of the climber's contrast stunningly with the crisp white of the fragrant tea roses. The gardener appears from behind a hedge, and he sees me standing there. I go to ask him to cut a rose for me, but he puts his head down and hurries away back into the depths of the woodland area. Oops, I remember that I'm in a bikini. Awkward.

"Victoria," my father calls me. I stroll back to the lounger and pick up my dressing gown. I've just finished wrapping it around me and tying the cord when he enters the room.

"Father." I smile.

"I've been looking for you everywhere."

"You know I *always* swim at this time," I offer with a hint of sarcasm, alluding to the fact that I don't have anything else to do.

"We don't have much time." He seems flustered.

"Time for what?" I come over to his side and place my arm through the crook of his. For all my father's overprotective faults, I do love him. I remember once, as a child, him building Theo and me this tent in his office and having afternoon tea with us in it. Theo, of course, being a lively boy wanted to use the shelter as a place to hide from the enemies who were chasing him. He didn't want to have a girly tea party, but my father insisted that it was my turn to choose the game, we sat with our pinkies out and pretended to drink tea.

"You have to get changed. We're going out."

"Out? Where?" I enquire with a great deal of excitement in my voice.

"It's time," he says and brushes me off, striding away through the house. I follow him as he heads toward my bedroom. Elsie's waiting in the room for us when we walk in. She looks sad. There's a definite air of tension in the room. Elsie steps aside and on the bed is a pure white linen dress. It's plain in design except for a small crest on the breast. I don't recognize it. Are those oak leaves? I try to think to whom it might belong but come up blank.

"Father, will you please tell me what's going on? I'm worried." I take his hand and squeeze it. He looks down at the floor.

"It's time for you to enter society. Put the dress on. No make-up. No undergarments. Just the dress. Elsie knows how your hair should be. We leave within the hour." I stand there in shock. Society? The door slams before I even realize he's left. I get to go and meet people. This is it — I finally get the freedom I crave. Alright, it'll be in probably the most unflattering dress I've ever seen, but at least it's going out. I squeal inwardly with barely contained excitement. My wish is going to come true.

Continuing reading at:
Amazon US: http://amzn.to/2FRo3fi
Bookbub: https://bit.ly/2vqksD5
Goodreads: http://bit.ly/GRLoS

I am a British author, from the depths of the rural country-side near London. In a previous life, I was an accountant from the age of twenty-one. I still do that on occasions, but most of my life is now spent intermingling writing while looking after my husband, two children, and two cats (probably in the inverse order to the one listed!). When I have some spare time, I can also be found writing poetry, baking cakes (and eating them), or behind a camera snapping like a mad paparazzi.

I'm an avid reader who turned to writing to combat my depression and anxiety. I have a love of travelling and like to bring this to my stories to give them the air of reality.

I like my heroes hot and hunky with a dirty mouth, my heroines demure but with spunk, and my books full of dramatic suspense.

www.AuthorAnnaEdwards.com

Newsletter: http://eepurl.com/cwxJ6v

Facebook, Author Page: AnnaEdwardsWriter

Facebook, Friend: TheAuthorAnnaEdwards

Twitter: Anna__Edwards

Instagram: AuthorAnnaEdwards

Pinterest: AuthorAnnaEdwards

Goodreads: Anna_Edwards

Bookbub: Anna-Edwards

Email: Anna1000Edwards@gmail.com

I'll be at the following signings:

2018

19-21 October – Shameless Book Convention, Showcase
Author, Orlando, Florida, USA.

10th November - Brighton Book Bash, Brighton, UK

2019

21-24 February - Wild Wicked Weekend, San Antonio,
Texas, USA

2nd March – Leeds Author Event, Leeds, UK

1st June – Heart of Steel, Sheffield, UK.

27th July – Books on the Beach, Blackpool, UK

Printed in Poland
by Amazon Fulfillment
Poland Sp. z o.o., Wrocław